COACH CARTER

D0446485

Coach Carter
© 2004 Paramount Pictures Corp.
HarperCollins®, ®, and HarperEntertainment
are trademarks of HarperCollins Publishers Inc.
All rights reserved. Printed in the U.S.A.
For information address HarperCollins Children's Books,
a division of HarperCollins Publishers,
1350 Avenue of the Americas, New York, NY 10019.
Library of Congress catalog card number: 2004108305
www.harperchildrens.com

1 2 3 4 5 6 7 8 9 10
❖
First Edition

COACH CARTER

ADAPTED BY JASMINE JONES
FROM THE SCREENPLAY WRITTEN BY
MARK SCHWAHN AND JOHN GATINS

HarperEntertainment
An Imprint of HarperCollins*Publishers*
Amistad

CHAPTER 1

"Test one two," a reporter said into his microphone as he stood before the battered walls of the Richmond High School gym. "St. Francis High School basketball phenom Ty Crane is widely hailed as the 'next LeBron James.' Most know him simply as 'the Crane.'"

On the court, the impossibly tall Crane yo-yoed the ball toward an exhausted Richmond player named Junior Battle. Junior's uniform was old and worn, soaked through with sweat, and provided a stark contrast to Ty Crane's crisp white St. Francis jersey. Pulling up, Ty launched a twenty-foot jumper. *Swish!* All net.

Ken Carter frowned as he stepped into the gym. This was the first preseason game of the year, and the bleachers were barely one-third full. The walls were a dingy shade of green, and a number of the scoreboard lights were burned out. He knew this gym well, and it was clearly the worse for wear.

Making his way to the St. Francis side of the bleachers, Carter took a seat next to his girlfriend, Tonya Wells, and glanced down at the bench, where the rest of the St. Francis team sat watching the game in their pristine white warm-ups. Carter glanced at the scoreboard. Richmond 32, Visitors 61.

Carter pressed his lips together. More than a full quarter to go, and this game was already over.

A weary Richmond guard chucked a lazy pass toward a teammate. Intercepted. Without looking, a St. Francis guard lobbed the ball toward the net. *Slam!* The Crane flew in and hammered the ball home, landing all over Junior.

"Stay out my way," Ty snarled. "I own you."

Junior shoved Crane, and in a moment, both teams swarmed their players. St. Francis formed a protective ring around Ty, while Richmond unleashed a series of punches and shoves that roused the security guards from the sidelines.

The ref looked at the coaches. "One quarter to go—" he said. "What do you want to do, guys?"

Coach White, who had led Richmond for the

past thirty years, looked up at the scoreboard and sighed. His players were frustrated by the beating they were taking, and he knew that the next conflict could cause an all out-brawl. "Let's call it," White said finally. "Thanks for the 'friendly' preseason game, Mike."

The St. Francis coach shook his head. "I'll never come down here again, Ray. Your boys don't need practice—" His eyes flashed as he looked at the Richmond team. "They need prison."

"Or maybe I need the St. Francis checkbook, so I can buy the best players in the country," Coach White snapped back. The ref stepped between the two men, but there was no need. White had said everything he had to say.

★★

Kenyon Stone tossed his filthy jersey into his locker. "Yo, Ty Crane outscored our whole team by himself," Kenyon said to no one in particular.

"We ain't had but thirty-two points," Junior pointed out. "I got twelve of 'em…what'd you get, Kenyon?"

"The Crane swooped down on you and delivered a large basket of beatdown…" The guard, Jason Lyle, grinned as he kidded Junior. Lyle was one of the only white players on the team. "Crane clowned you, dog. Kid had you on lock."

"Yo, Lyle," Timo Cruz put in as he adjusted his baggy pants, "if you don't shut your fat mouth, I'm gonna shut it for good."

"Can't we all just get along?" joked a scrawny kid named Worm.

Carter stood nearby, at the edge of the lockers, taking in the players. They didn't seem like much of a team to him. A sudden banging caught Carter's attention, and he looked over to see Coach White waving to him from his office window. Carter walked past the team.

"Kenny Ray Carter," Coach White said warmly as Carter walked into his office. "Richmond High School All-American, 1972."

Carter smiled and shook his old coach's hand. "Nice to see you, sir."

"I was really happy to see you in the stands tonight."

Carter held up a palm. "I have to tell you that I still haven't decided."

White nodded. "As I've told you, it's time for me to step down. Last few years have been really tough."

"Losing's hard," Carter said.

"This isn't about losing games, Kenny," White replied, the corners of his mouth twisting downward in frustration. "I can't get them to show up for school, for practice. I can't get parents involved. I'm done chasing kids in the street and pulling 'em into the gym."

Carter looked though the glass at the team. "This is a tough job."

"Richmond is a tough little city," White said. "You know that. What street are you on?"

"I live on Hillside," Carter replied. "But my sporting goods store's on Crawford."

"Then you know what I'm talkin' about. It's a challenge." The old coach chuckled. "When I saw you here tonight, I thought—'I got him. He's in.'"

"There's another reason I came tonight," Carter admitted. "My son plays for St. Francis."

White's eyebrows lifted in surprise. "He does? Which kid was he?"

"He didn't play," Carter said. "He's a freshman."

White nodded. "That's great," he said slowly. "It's a great school."

The front wall of the office shook as Cruz shoved Lyle against the glass. Coach White pounded the glass, and the players gave each other a final shove before shuffling away sheepishly. "You're seein' these boys on a bad night," White said, turning back to Carter. "They're frustrated." White folded his arms across his chest, as he looked Carter up and down. "Look at you, Kenny. You're the best thing to come out of Richmond basketball." He jerked his head toward the gym. "Your name's still on the wall out there."

"Playing basketball at Richmond was a really important part of my life," Carter admitted. "Still is."

"C'mon, Kenny," White pleaded, "you could do wonders here. I've officially offered you the job. That's it. I'll shut up now."

Carter heaved a sigh. He knew the truth—that if he could do wonders here, it was only because wonders needed to be done. On the other hand, it was a great opportunity to make a difference.... Carter looked up at his old coach, whose dark eyes were boring into him, eagerly trying to read his face. A slow smile spread across Carter's lips, and he nodded.

★★

"What's your name, boy? Urkel?" Worm taunted the African-American boy in the green suit jacket, gray slacks, and plaid green necktie. "Oh, I'm sorry, you play for St. Francis," Worm went on, his voice dripping sarcasm. "You must be the great Ty Crane."

Lyle leaned forward and whispered something in Worm's ear.

"Oh, I'm sorry," Worm said again, "I thought you were Ty Crane. See, the three black boys on St. Francis all look alike."

The boy stood still as the Richmond players hooted.

"So, son, how do you like Richmond?" Cruz asked in a low growl as he stepped up to the boy's face. "You scared of Richmond at night? You should be, son. You might have won the game, but you lucky they stopped the fight."

Without speaking, Carter stepped into the circle and led away his son.

The Richmond players strolled off. "Daddy, save me! Save me!" one of them mocked as the others laughed and slapped high-fives.

"What was that about?" Carter asked his son.

Damien Carter shook his head as he and his father walked toward the bleachers where Tonya was chatting with another parent. "Nothing."

Tonya looked up at Carter as Damien walked past and onto the court. "What did you tell him?" she whispered.

Carter shook his head. "I'll tell you later," he said in a low voice.

Tonya and Carter joined Damien at the free throw line, where he stood looking up at an All-American blanket on the wall behind the basket. "Ken Carter All-American 1971 and 1972?" Damien read aloud, looking up at his dad. "Both years?"

"Yes, sir, both years," Carter said. "I played with a great team."

"Were the baskets ten feet high back then?" he asked, barely managing to keep a straight face as he teased his father. "They must have been nine feet. Or maybe it was co-ed? Were you playing against girls?"

The corner of Carter's mouth ticked up into a smile, and he lunged at Damien, who tried to dodge away. The two grappled playfully as they made their way toward the exit. Tonya grinned at them, wondering what Carter had told Coach White.

★★

"I can't coach that team," Carter insisted later that

evening as he paced through the kitchen of his modest one-story house. "Did you see those kids?"

"What about Damien?" Tonya asked.

"He's asleep."

"No, Kenny." Tonya shook her head. "I mean, how would Damien feel if you coached at Richmond?"

"I don't know," Carter admitted. Thinking a moment, he added, "He'd be upset."

"So you told the coach 'no.'" Tonya's face held a question.

"No," Carter replied slowly. "I told him I'd think about it. But you saw the school," he went on, as though he was trying to convince himself. "It was rough when I went there, but it's beyond that now."

Tonya shrugged. "Then forget it, Kenny. Don't even discuss it again."

"I have to," Carter said impatiently, "he officially offered me the job tonight. I'm on the clock."

Tonya looked at him evenly. "And when you say 'offer' and 'job,' there's usually money involved."

Carter smiled. "I'm sure there's a thousand dollars in it for me."

"For five months' work?" Tonya's eyes were round. "Well...you can't say no to that," she joked.

"And the team is bad," Carter added, "the players are angry—"

"You don't have the time," Tonya pointed out. "You're trying to open a second store—"

"That's right. I don't have the time." Carter nodded vehemently. "I don't have any time."

"And you promised to take your girlfriend to Mexico in January—" Tonya added.

"Exactly, and we're goin', baby. I promise. That's what I'm sayin'," Carter went on, "I cannot take this job."

Tonya and Carter looked at each other for a moment. They were in perfect agreement.

"So," Tonya said finally, "when do you start?"

Carter smiled and shook his head. He had known from the beginning that Tonya would understand. She always did. "They would need me right away."

Tonya smiled as she grabbed a pile of papers off the kitchen table and shoved them into her sleek black briefcase.

Carter eyed the bag. "You goin' home?"

"I have to be at the hospital early tomorrow," Tonya explained. "Thanks for dinner." She stopped on her way out of the kitchen to give Carter a gentle kiss. "You're going to be a great coach, Kenny," she said in a quiet voice. She kissed him again, then smiled.

Carter heaved a sigh as Tonya walked out the door.

He hoped she was right.

CHAPTER 2

"What happens to me?" Damien asked the next morning as he sat in his father's battered Mercedes, which was idling in front of the pristine St. Francis exterior. "My games? Are you still gonna come to my games?"

"I'll probably miss most of your games," Carter admitted, not bothering to point out that it wouldn't make much of a difference, considering that Damien was mostly a bench-warmer.

Damien rubbed his sweaty palms against his gray wool slacks. "Then I'll go to Richmond and play for you," he said.

Carter shook his head.

"Why not?" Damien demanded. "You've always been my coach."

Carter's eyes flicked to the elegant St. Francis façade. "You know this is a great school that puts you in a great position for college."

"Dad, I—"

"My coaching at Richmond does not change our plans for your future," Carter said.

Damien set his jaw. He knew that there was no point in arguing with his father. Instead, he got out of the car and slammed the door in frustration. He hated St. Francis. No one from the neighborhood went there, and Damien felt conspicuous.

Carter watched as his son disappeared into the crowd of prep school kids streaming into the school. He was right about this—he was sure of it. He just hoped that Damien understood.

★★

"Nice to see you again, Mr. Carter." Principal Garrison, an officious looking African-American woman. She exuded a commanding presence from behind her desk as Carter stepped into her office. Coach White stood beside her, grinning.

"Ma'am, if the offer stands," Carter said, "I'd like to coach the team."

Ms. Garrison nodded thoughtfully. "I hope you're up for the task. These young men need discipline. The job comes with a fifteen hundred dollar stipend and a major time commitment for the next four months."

Carter nodded. "I accept."

Principal Garrison seemed only mildly surprised at Carter's words. "Great. We're thrilled to have you." She stood up, signaling that the meeting was over. "Not to be abrupt, Mr. Carter, but I do have to run to a budget meeting. So, is there anything you need from us?"

Carter handed over the single page he'd spent all night drafting and re-drafting. "Ma'am, all I need is about twenty-five copies of this document, and I'm all set."

Ms. Garrison handed the sheet to Coach White. "Ray, see that Mr. Carter—Coach Carter," she corrected herself, smiling apologetically, "gets these copies." She turned back to Carter. "Thank you. It's nice to have a Richmond graduate. Good luck."

★ ★

The gym echoed with the sound of trash talk and the squeak of sneakers on hardwood as Carter and Coach White walked toward the players. A few were shooting baskets, while the rest lounged on the first row of bleachers. It looked to Carter as though half of the team hadn't bothered to show up yet.

"Guys, guys. GUYS!" White shouted as he and Carter stepped into the gym. The players turned to face him, still murmuring and elbowing each other. "As you know, I've been looking for a new coach to take over for me," White announced. He motioned toward Carter. "This is Ken Carter. He went to Richmond. He was a two-time All-American, and still holds records for scoring, assists, and steals. He received a basketball scholarship to George Mason University. We are lucky to have Coach Carter. Let's show him the respect he deserves." White turned to Carter. "They're all yours," he said in a low voice, grinning.

Carter shook White's hand, then stood beside a desk ten feet from the bleachers as he waited for his old coach to leave. The Richmond players weren't paying attention to him. Not that he minded. He knew they'd pay attention soon enough.

Once his watch showed 2:55, Carter straightened his already perfect tie and turned to the players. "Good afternoon, young men," he announced. "As Coach White said, I am Ken Carter, your new basketball coach."

None of the players even turned in his direction.

They continued roughhousing and trash-talking, acting as though Carter was a substitute teacher.

Carter cleared his throat. "You obviously can't hear me," he said, his voice rising to a drill-sergeant shout, "so I *will speak louder to get your attention*!"

The gym fell silent as the players turned to look at their new coach. Worm was the first to swagger forward. "Yo, we can *hear* you," he quipped, "but we can't *see* you. There's too much glare comin' off that shiny head of yours." The team cracked up behind him. "Yo, ya head is mad bright!" Worm went on. "Do you buff it?"

"Yes, sir," Carter said smoothly. "I buff it every morning with Turtle Wax." Giving Worm a cool look, he added, "Now, if you want to check my other credentials, they are on the wall behind you."

Most of the players didn't bother to turn and look, but a few of them swiveled to see the All-American blanket and record banner.

"If practice is at three, then you are late as of two fifty-five," Carter announced. He turned to one of the players who was flopped on the bleachers. "What is your name, sir?"

Lyle gave Carter a lopsided grin. "Jason Lyle," he said. "But I ain't no *sir*."

"Not a sir?" Carter's eyebrows flew up. "Are you a madam?" A few of the players snickered at the dis. "As of today, you are a sir," Carter went on. "Sir is a term of respect. You will have my respect until you abuse it. Sit up, sir. How many games did this team win last year?"

Lyle shrugged. "We was four wins, twenty-two losses."

"Sir," Carter prompted.

Lyle nodded, still grinning cockily. "Sir."

"In my hand, I hold a contract." Carter held up the stack of white papers for everyone to see. "If you sign this contract and honor your side of it, we are going to be successful."

"Do I get a signing bonus?" Worm cracked.

"Yes, sir," Carter replied, "you get to become a winner. Because if there's one thing I'm sure of, it's this: The losing stops now. Starting today, you will learn to play like winners, act like winners, and most of all—be winners. If you listen and learn, you will win basketball games. And gentlemen...winning in here is the key to winning out there." Carter gestured beyond the walls of the gym as he weaved through the players, handing out contracts. "This contract states that you will maintain a two point three grade point average, you will attend all classes, and you will sit in the front row of all your classes. You will be better members of this community. You will wear a tie on all game days—"

"He a country nigga," Worm muttered to Cruz.

Around him, the players busted out laughing. Carter stopped in his tracks, then wheeled to face Worm. "Did you say something, sir?" he demanded. "Sir? What's your name?"

Worm didn't reply, but Cruz stood slowly, narrowing his eyes at the new coach. "Timo Cruz, sir," he said in a low growl. He gestured to Worm. "Worm was wondering...are you, like, some country church nigga—with yo tie on an' all that?"

Carter's eyes flashed dangerously. "Well, Mr. Cruz and Mr. Worm," he said coldly, "you should both know that we treat ourselves with respect. And we don't use the word nigger."

Cruz didn't flinch. "Are you a preacher man, or somethin'?" he demanded. "Well, God ain't gonna do you no good in this neighborhood."

"I live in this neighborhood, sir," Carter replied.

"Sir?" Cruz scoffed. He turned to his teammates. "Can you believe this uppity negro?"

"Mr. Cruz, please leave this gym right now," Carter said.

Cruz didn't move.

Carter stepped right up to him. "Sir, I will ask you one last time to leave before I help you leave!" he shouted.

Cruz's eyes were cold as he stepped forward, halving the distance between himself and the coach. "Do you know who I am?" he snarled.

Carter nodded. "A very scared and confused young man..."

"Scared?" Cruz demanded, sneering. "I ain't scared of no one. I'll lay you out."

Carter didn't blink. "Try me."

The players stared as the two faced off, neither moving, neither speaking. Finally, sensing that the moment had passed, Carter turned away. Cruz jumped on the opportunity, swinging at the coach. Like lightning, Carter deflected the blow with his forearm, then dodged Cruz's second punch. Grabbing Cruz in a headlock, Carter hurled him to the ground, then grabbed the hood of his sweatshirt and yanked him up, pressing Cruz against the wall.

"Teachers ain't supposed to touch students," Cruz snarled between heavy breaths.

Carter yanked Cruz away from the wall and shoved him toward the door. "I'm not a teacher," Carter barked. "I'm the new basketball coach."

Cruz took a few stumbling steps, then recovered. He yanked down his sweatshirt, straightening it. "This ain't over," he warned. Then he turned and walked through the gym doors.

Carter turned back to face his team. "If there is anyone else that doesn't want to agree to this..." he said, indicating the contract.

Two players turned and headed for the exit. With a grin at the new coach, one of them tossed his crumpled contract on the ground. "You tell us when you need the best ballers," the player said.

"I will let you know, sir," Carter replied.

Kenyon shook his head as he watched the players leave. "There goes our two leading scorers from last season."

Carter gave him a cool look. "Then I guess we'll have new leading scorers this year." After a moment, Carter went on, "A parent or guardian must attend a meeting to discuss and sign these contracts on Thursday night at seven." Carter straightened his shirt and tie. "I cannot teach you the game of basketball until your conditioning is at a level that allows me to do so. Gentlemen, report to the baseline."

The players exchanged *Is-he-serious?* glances.

"Gentlemen, to the baseline!" Carter shouted.

The teammates straggled to the baseline.

"I presume you know what suicides are," Carter said, folding his arms across his chest.

The players eyed each other dubiously. Sure—they knew what suicides were: touch the free throw line, then the half line, and then full court. Nobody wanted to run suicides.

"I saw the St. Francis game and *none* of you had a problem shooting the basketball," Carter explained. "*All* of you had a problem running up and down the court. If you are late, you will run. If you give me attitude, you will do push-ups. So you can shut up or push-up, it is your choice—"

Kenyon gave the coach a smug smile. "Yo, how many we gonna do?"

"Sir?" Carter added.

"Yo, sir," Kenyon corrected himself, "how many we gonna do?"

"It's up to you, sir," Carter replied. "How many can you do in..." He checked his watch. "One hour and seven minutes?"

CHAPTER 3

Hamburger Dan's was jumping as Worm, Kenyon, and Maddux hobbled in, trying to hide the stiffness in their legs.

"He can't keep this up," Kenyon griped. "I can barely walk."

Worm nudged Kenyon, grinning hugely. "There's your shorty..."

Kenyon followed Worm's glance and spotted his girlfriend, Kyra, walking toward him with her two best friends, Dominique and Peyton.

"Ladies," Worm said brightly, eyeing Kyra's posse, "two-for-one special. Two of you—one of me." He waggled his eyebrows. "Now that's special."

"Yeah," Dominique snapped back, cracking her gum. "Special ed."

Worm corralled the girls into a three-way bear hug. "Get off me, Worm!" Peyton complained, screeching with laughter.

Kenyon laughed as Kyra tipped her face to kiss him. "I got somethin' for the baby today," she whispered, pulling an adorable pair of baby-sized Nikes from her purse.

Kenyon's smile vanished. "We don't know if it's a baby yet," he said. "I mean, it's early...you ain't even been to a doctor..."

"Hel-*lo*?" Kyra looked up at him, a smile playing at the corners of her mouth. "I passed the pregnancy test, Kenyon. Three times."

Kenyon nodded, but somehow he couldn't come up with a smile.

"What's wrong?" Kyra asked, reading his expression.

Kenyon draped his arm around her shoulders. He wished that he could be as excited about the baby as Kyra was...but he just didn't feel it. He didn't want to tell her that, though. "Nothin'," he said finally. He guided her into a corner and leaned in close, his hand pressed against the wall. "I got Coach Carter breathin' down my neck about my grades, and stuff." He took the tiny Nikes from her hand and smiled at them. "These are tight, though."

Kyra gave him a sly smile. "I got somethin' for you, too." She looked around, then pulled a miniscule thong from her purse.

"Yo," Kenyon said, his eyes growing wide, "that definitely is a *little* something."

Kyra giggled. "Not bad for the ninety-nine cent store, huh?"

Kenyon lifted his eyebrows. "How many did you get for ninety-nine cent? Ninety-nine?"

Kyra shoved him playfully.

"Girl, I been in there," Kenyon went on. "You can get, like, three brooms and a bucket for ninety-nine cent. This like half a shoelace with thread."

Smiling, Kyra pulled him close and whispered, "Would you like to see me in this shoelace?"

"Oh, yeah," Kenyon said huskily. He leaned in and kissed her, the baby Nikes dangling from his fingertips.

* *

Damien dribbled the ball, then tried to pull a quick crossover move. No good. With a laser-fast slap, Carter picked it clean.

"How many times are you gonna cross me over?" Carter demanded. "You haven't moved me one inch." He gestured to the two square feet of driveway that Damien had owned all evening. "That's pretty for the camera, but on the court, you need to know when to use it." Motioning for his son to dribble toward him, Carter added, "Make him commit one way."

Damien dribbled to his father's right.

"Now!" Carter shouted.

Crossing over, Damien made his move.

"Bam," Carter hooted. "You got him! Better, much better. We're done." He reached for a towel as Damien headed inside.

A moment later, Carter joined his son in the kitchen.

Damien took a deep breath. "Why didn't you ask St. Francis if you could help coach?" he asked his father slowly. "I mean, you didn't even consider it."

Carter knew that St. Francis didn't need any help ...but those Richmond players needed all the help they could get. "Damien," Carter said patiently, "I'm coaching at Richmond."

"You should have spoken to me first," Damien said, scowling.

"It was a personal decision for me."

Damien looked at his father for a moment. "I want to go to Richmond," he said finally.

Carter shook his head. "Richmond's not good enough for you."

"It was good enough for *you*," Damien shot back.

"I had no choice."

"You making me go to St. Francis doesn't feel like a choice," Damien pointed out.

"Damien—"

"If I've got a choice," Damien interrupted, "I choose Richmond."

"Okay," Carter replied, "you don't have a choice."

"Why would you coach at Richmond and then not let me go there and play for you?" Damien demanded, his voice rising in frustration.

"We worked hard to get you into St. Francis," Carter snapped, losing patience. "This is not about basketball, it's about your life. It's about your life after basketball."

Clenching his jaw, Damien turned and walked out of the kitchen. This conversation was over, and he knew it.

And, as usual, his father hadn't heard a word he'd said.

★★

"Sir," Carter announced from his place at the baseline the following day as Junior straggled into the gym, "you are twenty minutes late. That's ten suicides for the entire team and two hundred fifty push-ups for you."

The team let out a collective groan.

"This ain't the track team," Lyle griped.

"Nor is it the debate club," Carter snapped, stepping up to Lyle. "You're right, Mr. Lyle, and because you're right, the team will now run *twenty* suicides and you can join Mr. Battle with two hundred fifty push-ups of your own."

"This is crap," Junior complained.

"Right you are, Mr. Battle. Johnny, tell him what he's won!" Carter added in a gameshow announcer's voice. "Five hundred push-ups, Mr. Battle! Would you like to try for a thousand?"

Silence rang through the gym.

"Gentlemen, on my whistle," Carter announced.

The players stepped up to the baseline and took off at the whistle's screech. "You are a team!" Carter shouted as the players ran. "If one player struggles, the whole team struggles. If one player triumphs, we all triumph."

★★

Lyle and Worm were limping home when a black Nissan Maxima cut them off, screeching to a halt.

Lyle tried to run, but a thug grabbed him and shoved him against a wall, shoving a gun to his head. "Run your shit!" the thug shouted.

"Take it!" Lyle cried. "Take my bag!"

With that, the thug started laughing. Turning, Lyle realized it was none other than Cruz—his former teammate.

"What's the matter with you? You crazy, Cruz?" Lyle snapped. "I'll visit you in county."

"I'm just playin'," Cruz said, grinning. "Look at you. I seen you from up the block—walkin' like someone put a pipe in ya asses. I can't believe you playin' for him." Cruz slapped hands with his thug friend, and eyed the .45 in his hand. "I should put a hole in Coach Carter. For real, we weren't good when I was there, but without me, y'all is straight sad." He let out a chuckle. "I'ma come watch you get your asses kicked, too."

The driver's side door opened, and an older boy got out. Lyle swallowed hard. It was Renny, Cruz's cousin. He was a drug dealer, and notorious in the neighborhood.

"I'd love to shoot the breeze with you all day," Renny said cheerfully, "but I gotta go."

Cruz nodded respectfully.

"Who dat?" Worm asked.

"My cousin, Renny," Cruz said. "Yo, Worm, you wanna ride?"

Worm shook his head, eyeing the Nissan warily. "Nah, I'm straight."

Worm and Cruz hugged lightly and knocked fists as Lyle stormed away, still pissed about Cruz's "practical joke."

"All right, Lyle," Cruz called after him. "Don't let that coach put anything else up your ass..." Cruz grinned wickedly and mimed leaning against an imaginary wall. "Take my bag!" he mimicked. "Take me, too! Take me!"

Lyle didn't even turn back. Cruz shot the finger at his retreating form.

★★

Carter stood at the front of the classroom like a boulder at the center of a hurricane. Around him, furious parents were shouting and waving contracts.

"But the state only requires that they have a two point oh average to play!" barked a woman standing beside Junior. "You got in here that they need a two point three!"

Cries of agreement rose from the parents behind her.

"With a two point oh, you need to score a ten-fifty on the S.A.T. to be eligible for an athletic scholarship," Carter explained calmly. "With a two point three, you only need nine hundred and fifty. A two point three is a C plus—it shouldn't be hard to maintain a C plus. These are *student* athletes. Student comes first."

"It says they gotta wear a coat and tie on game days," blustered a player's uncle. "They don't own ties. How they gonna buy ties?"

Carter raised his hand as the crowd began shouting in agreement.

"There is a Goodwill and a Salvation Army store less than two blocks from where we're standing," Carter explained. "They have a box of ties for fifty cents each."

The parents reacted, grumbling loudly.

Carter lifted an eyebrow. "I know we're all too good to shop at the Salvation Army."

"This is crazy!" Junior's mom shouted. "A dress code, and they have to sit in the front row at class—this is *basketball*!"

"Yes, and basketball is a *privilege*!" Carter shot

back, finally losing patience. "If you want to play basketball on this team, these are the simple rules you must obey to enjoy this *privilege.*"

The room fell silent under the power of Carter's words.

"If you decide to follow these rules, sign it, and bring it to practice tomorrow." Gathering his things, Carter turned and left the room as the parents continued to gripe behind him.

That had actually gone better than he had expected.

★★

Carter was sitting down at his kitchen table to enjoy a slice of pie when Damien entered and dropped a piece of paper in front of him.

"It's one of your contracts—" Damien explained.

Carter picked up the paper. "So it is."

"I've amended that contract, sir. You require your players to maintain a two point three grade point average," Damien said as his father squinted at the scribbled changes he had made to the contract. "I have committed to maintaining a three point five. You require ten hours of community service. I have committed to fifty. Any unexcused absences, detentions, or other disciplinary issues at school—you can nullify this agreement and send me to any school you want."

Carter looked up at his son and was surprised by the seriousness in his eyes. "How many days do I have to respond to this offer?"

"None," Damien replied. "The last page is a letter you need to sign that confirms my withdrawal from St. Francis. They know I'm leaving."

"*What?*" Carter cried. "You withdrew from St. Francis?"

"And I called Richmond today," Damien added. "They expect me there in the morning."

"You called Richmond?" Carter repeated in disbelief. "You should have spoken to me first!"

Damien's face was impassive. "There's a lot of that going around."

"We're gonna fix this all in the morning," Carter said, staring at the papers in his hand.

"Sir, please listen. All I want to do is play for you. And if I'm one of the top students at Richmond, one of the top in the whole school, and I have great S.A.T.s—I can go to any college in the country. I'm asking you to trust me."

Carter looked up at his son's pleading face. He

couldn't hide the fury he was feeling. "You really wanna do this?" Carter demanded. "Part of growing up is making your own choices and dealing with the results."

Damien nodded with determination.

With a frustrated sigh, Carter looked down at the contract. He noted something in the margin before signing it. "three point seven," he said finally. "And you will earn every minute of playing time."

A grin broke out over Damien's face. "Yes, sir."

CHAPTER 4

"Dad," Damien said as his father's old Mercedes rolled up to the front of the school, "let me out here."

"Damien, I have to go inside, anyway. I can walk you—"

"I'll be fine," Damien assured him.

Sighing, Carter stopped the car and looked over at his son doubtfully.

"What?" Damien asked, looking down at his crisp clothes. "This is very nice." He patted his tie. "I look nice, you don't think this is nice?"

Carter smiled ruefully. "Nice enough to be buried in it."

Damien gave his father an embarrassed smile. "I can't believe you're on me for dressing well. What are you so worried about?"

"Son, this is Richmond...the *teachers* don't wear ties."

"This is how I dress," Damien insisted. He opened the door and stepped out.

Carter stared at the heavens, hoping that someone would protect his son.

★★

"I'm a mad rapper, yo," Lyle bragged as he held court in the middle of the hall. "I got skills to pay the bills, y'all."

"Hope your bills are cheap," Kenyon said, slapping Junior a high-five.

"That's cold-blooded, yo," Worm said.

Junior gave Worm a playful shove.

"Lay it down, man," Junior urged Lyle. "Let's hear it."

Lyle didn't need more of an invitation than that to start busting his rhymes. "My name is J Lyle, I told y'all I'm wild..." Lyle stopped mid-flow, and his eyes widened.

"Yo," Worm called, spotting Damien, "it's Malcolm X!"

Damien looked over, confused. He was holding a map of the school.

"Yo, Malcolm," Worm shouted. "What's up, Malcolm?"

"What are you doing here?" Lyle demanded as

the players crowded around Damien.

"I transferred to Richmond," Damien replied.

"Oh, no, no, no, son," Junior said, wagging his head. "I think you're just lost."

"I *am* actually lost," Damien admitted, "can you tell me how to get to—"

"Bel-Air?" Kenyon finished for him. "Lyle, tell the fresh prince here how to get to Bel-Air."

The friends cracked up as the late bell sounded. Kenyon and Lyle sauntered off as Lyle stared Damien down. "I hope seein' you in this hallway means I'ma see you on the court today," he said sharply. "I can't wait."

★ ★

"Mrs. Fenton, the police are telling a different story," a very harassed-looking Principal Garrison said into the phone as she waved Carter into her office. She nodded at the unseen Mrs. Fenton. "I wish you would. Yes, ma'am, I'm here every day." Hanging up the phone, the principal looked up. "Mr. Carter, how are the boys?"

"Ma'am, our first game's this Friday."

"Very good." Placing her hands in her lap, Garrison leaned back and gave Carter a level look.

"How may I help you?"

"Ma'am, I had my boys sign contracts that required them to meet certain academic standards," Carter began.

Garrison pursed her lips thoughtfully. "I think one of the faculty mentioned that. That was an interesting scare tactic, sir."

"Ma'am, to be successful, teachers need to fill out a weekly progress report to let me know how my players are doing in the classroom." Carter gazed at her expectantly.

Garrison gave her head a slight shake. "Okay—" she prompted.

"Well, ma'am," Carter went on, "I've yet to receive any response from their teachers."

"I'm not sure how this ties into your job as the basketball coach," Garrison said, narrowing her eyes.

"I took this job with the understanding that I could do this my way."

Garrison eyed the coach, as though she was sizing him up. "And you can," she said finally. "Our next faculty meeting is in two weeks. I'll remember to bring it up."

Carter knew that he wasn't likely to get a bigger commitment, so he decided to let it go. "That'd be great," Carter said. "Thank you, ma'am."

★ ★

"Okay," Carter announced as the players stretched out around him, "today we will play defense."

Just then, Damien raced into the gym, still in his blazer and tie. Carter blinked at his son, then turned to the rest of the team. "This is a new player," Carter announced, "Damien Carter. He is my son, and he is late. Sir," he said, turning to Damien, "you owe me twenty suicides."

Damien gaped at his father in disbelief. "Sir, it's my first day of school. I had to stay and talk to my math—"

"Practice starts at three," Carter said evenly. "You are late as of two fifty-five. Get changed and do those suicides on the far side of the court so as not to disturb us."

Damien stood still for a moment, as though he thought perhaps his father was joking. But when not even a flicker of a smile crossed Carter's face, Damien turned toward the locker room to get changed while the rest of the team snickered.

"Gentlemen!" Carter shouted. When the team had

quieted down, he went on. "Everything you need to know about basketball, I learned from women."

The players looked at each other in confusion as Carter nodded knowingly. "Man, I have a sister named Diane, and growing up, she would never back down. She was on me about every last little thing—'turn down that radio!'" Carter mocked, mimicking his sister's high-pitched squeal. "'Don't eat the last piece of cake!' She would just get in my face!" Carter chuckled as the Richmond players exchanged questioning glances. "When I call 'Diane!' we will play straight man-to-man pressure defense," he explained. "Now, there was Delilah," Carter went on. "She was my childhood sweetheart."

"Sir," Maddux asked with a wicked grin, "was she hot?"

Carter nodded. "She was. But that little girl was tricky. Delilah tricked me into stealing a brownie from the Christ the King Baptist Church bake sale. And when I got caught, she smiled her way out of it and I mopped the church for a month." Carter narrowed his eyes. "Delilah could trick you into anything."

Worm and Lyle exchanged a smile.

"Delilah is our trap defense," Carter went on. "Allow one pass, and then trap the ball. That's Delilah. Skins on D," Carter instructed. "Shirts inbound. Delilah!"

The skins allowed one pass, then trapped the ball-handler, forcing a tie-up.

"Maddux," Carter bellowed, "you're late getting over there! Where do we want to force the ball?"

"Uh...um...the corner?" Maddux guessed.

"You don't sound so sure," Carter said.

"Yes, sir," Maddux replied. "I mean, no..." He shook his head. "I mean yes."

Carter cocked an eyebrow. "It can't be both."

"Yes," Maddux said with greater certainty. "We're forcing it to the corner."

"That's right, gentlemen," Carter said as Maddux heaved a sigh of relief. "Use that sideline as your third defender," Carter went on. "Good things happen when we trap in the corner. Let's go! Ball up top!"

The team ran the drill a few more times, until Lyle stopped the play. "So," he said, "Diane is full court man-to-man, Delilah, I'm allowing one pass and then I trap."

"Yes, sir, yes sir." Carter nodded vigorously. "Now,

let's see you run it in full court. Junior, Lyle, Kenyon, Worm, and Maddux, go skins. Ball up top!"

Worm checked the ball at the top of the key, then yanked it away as Damien reached for it. "Take notes, freshman," Worm taunted. "This is as close as you're gonna get to playin'."

Carter's whistle screamed through the gym. "Diane!" the coach shouted, and the skins snapped into straight man-to-man defense.

His plan was working already.

★ ★

"Malcolm," Worm taunted Damien as the players dressed for their first official game, "you ain't gonna get any run, so you could be bare-ass naked under those sweats."

Kenyon and Lyle cracked up as Carter walked past the group. He gave Junior a cold stare. "I noticed you weren't in the front row of your science class today," Carter whispered fiercely. "I'm sure you just forgot."

Reading the cold fire in the coach's eyes, Junior nodded wordlessly.

"Gentlemen," Carter said, raising his voice so the entire team could hear, "circle up, please. I know that you are concerned that we didn't work on our offense in practice. We have all season for that."

Kenyon bit his lip as he gave Worm a sideways look. He *had* been worried about that.

"What did we do in practice?" Carter demanded. He turned and looked Kenyon in the eye. "Mr. Stone—"

"Run?" Kenyon guessed.

"Run, yes, sir. What are we gonna do on offense, sir?"

Kenyon thought for a moment. "Run?"

Carter smiled. "Yes, sir," he said slowly, "we're gonna run. We're gonna run on defense, too. All day long. Every second that clock is ticking, we're pressing on defense. When we have the ball, we're moving. Keep it simple. It's early in the season. We push the tempo of this game, and we will cook this team. Young men, the journey of a thousand miles begins with the first step. Tonight we take that step...hands in..."

Each of the Richmond players placed a hand at the center of the circle. "Run on three..." Carter said. "One, two, three—"

"Run!" the team shouted as their hands flew up and they hauled out of the locker room.

Carter smiled after them. Let the games begin, he thought.

★ ★

The sparse crowd was quiet as the game began. Nestled on the bleachers of the opposing school, former Richmond player Cruz watched the game coolly. Hercules gained control of the ball first, but Worm pressed in, grabbing the steal and laying it in for two. The Hercules team wasn't going to lie down that easy, however. Grabbing the rebound, one of the guards drove through Richmond's full-court press and hit an eight-foot jumper.

The teams were evenly matched, but Richmond pressed harder, running on defense, running on offense, running, running, their now-solid legs holding them. True, they hadn't practiced their offense. But their D was strong, and their conditioning was excellent. Still, by the end of the fourth quarter, they were down by six with fifty-seven seconds to go.

If he was nervous, Carter didn't show it as he surveyed his team with a gaze of steel. "Junior," he commanded during the time-out, "move your feet. We're okay. Let's keep pushing it."

Damien watched his teammates hustle out onto the court from his place on the bench, wishing desperately that he could do something to help the team.

At the whistle, Richmond inbounded to Worm, who penetrated the Hercules defense. He passed to Kenyon, who hit the jumper from downtown. Now they were down by three.

Richmond set up Delilah, and Maddux reached in on a Hercules guard as they inbounded the ball. A whistle tore through the air.

"That's his fifth foul, Coach," the ref called, pointing to Maddux.

"Time out, sir," Carter said, grimacing as Maddux flopped heavily onto the bench. Carter looked over at his remaining players. "Mr. Carter," he said to his son.

Jumping up, Damien peeled off his sweats. The already-huddled players exchanged angry looks.

"C'mon man," Worm griped, "he's a freshman."

Damien blew into his hands nervously. He could feel the doubt radiating from Worm, Junior, Kenyon, and Lyle.

"Listen to me," Carter said, glancing at the six-foot-ten Hercules guard. "This guy is dead tired.

COACH KEN CARTER

THE RICHMOND OILERS MEET THEIR NEW COACH.

RICHMOND OILERS

MRS. WORM TAKES ONE FOR THE TEAM.

SERIOUS TRAINING WHIPS THE OILERS INTO SHAPE.

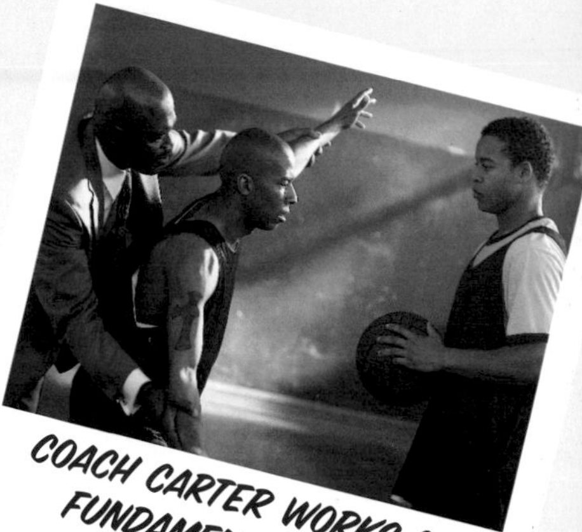

COACH CARTER WORKS ON FUNDAMENTALS WITH KENYON AND DAMIEN.

ON THE WAY TO A WIN, DAMIEN TAKES IT UPCOURT.

OFF THE COURT, CRUZ'S COUSIN RENNY GIVES HIM A PIECE OF HIS MIND.

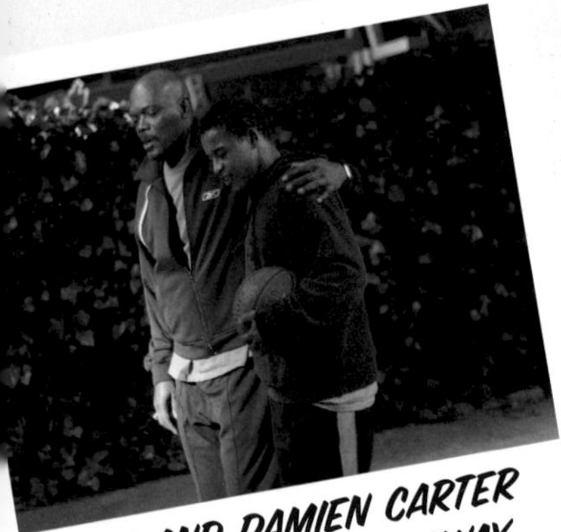

KEN AND DAMIEN CARTER SHARE A MOMENT AWAY FROM THE TEAM.

THIS TEAM IS UNSTOPPABLE!

RICHMOND OILERS

THE UNDEFEATED OILERS.

FREMONT
GAME
HAS BEEN
CANCELLED

AS FAR AS THEIR COACH IS CONCERNED, THERE WILL BE NO MORE BASKETBALL AT RICHMOND HIGH UNTIL THE PLAYERS IMPROVE THEIR GRADES.

THE COMMUNITY SHOWS COACH CARTER HOW THEY FEEL ABOUT THE LOCKOUT.

THE COACH DEFENDS HIS POLICY—GRADES COME BEFORE BASKETBALL.

THE PLAYERS SUPPORT THEIR COACH AND REFUSE TO PLAY.

THE OILERS ARE BACK IN TIME TO FACE THEIR LONGTIME RIVAL, ST. FRANCIS.

COACH CARTER PUMPS UP HIS TEAM: "LEAVE EVERYTHING ON THIS COURT."

When he misses, Lyle and Worm are our first two options. Push it, take it strong to the hole. Everyone crashes the boards. Richmond on three. One, two, three…"

"Richmond!" The team trotted to their places along the foul line.

Just as Carter predicted, the Hercules guard missed his shot. Kenyon grabbed the rebound and eyed Lyle and Worm—both were covered. Like lightning, Damien cut to the ball, and Kenyon slammed him a last-ditch rocket. Damien powered upcourt, dribbling through two defenders and streaking toward the basket. In a quick, fluid motion, he dodged the defender and drove hard to the hoop. The six-foot-ten defender swatted at the ball—too late. The pretty little floater kissed the glass and swished through the net.

"Diane!" Carter shouted as the Richmond bench exploded. "Diane!"

They were down by one with sixteen seconds left. Richmond swarmed the exhausted Hercules offense. The inbounder tried to hit a long pass, but Kenyon broke on the ball, intercepting it, and pushing it quickly downcourt, where Damien was open.

Damien headed for the baseline, trailed by two defenders. He took them airborne, aiming for the jumper—but instead of shooting, he fired a no-look pass to Worm, who was alone under the basket. Worm banked the easy layup as the crowd went wild.

"Nice pass, D!" Worm shouted, slapping Damien's hand. "That was all you, man!"

The players punched the air in victory, shouting and hooting as though they had just won the Olympic gold. Even Carter let loose—with a tiny smile—as he shook the hand of the Hercules coach.

Victory had never tasted so sweet.

CHAPTER 5

"They looked much bigger, too," Tonya said later that night as she and Carter sat in the living room, sipping coffee.

"Tonya, they were bigger at every position," Carter replied, barely able to contain his joy. "Center was six-foot-ten." He looked up as Damien appeared in the doorway. "Where you goin', young man?"

Damien hesitated. "With Kenyon, Lyle, and them—"

"*Them* who, son?" Carter demanded. "Speak up."

"The team," Damien explained. "They're all hangin' out. They asked me to meet up."

Carter gave his son a disapproving frown. "I don't think so, Damien. It's already after nine. Where they goin'?"

"I dunno," Damien admitted, "but we're supposed

to meet at Hamburger Dan's on Division."

"And then where?"

Damien winced. "I'm not sure. I can call you—"

"No." Carter's voice was firm, but not unkind. "I'm sorry, Damien—"

"Tonya," Damien said, pleading with his father's girlfriend, "don't you think it's okay?"

Carter's expression darkened. "We're not gonna argue about this."

"C'mon, Dad," Damien begged. "Let me just go for an hour. I'll be back before eleven."

"Kenny—" Tonya interjected, but Carter cut her off.

"No."

"Why not?" Damien demanded.

"You're not going to hang out on the street on Friday night looking for something to do," Carter insisted. "That's a bad plan."

Damien's eyes narrowed to angry slits. "Do you really think that I'm gonna go out there and do something stupid?"

"No," Carter said gently, "I don't. I'm not worried about what you do. My experience tells me that stupid things happen out there."

"You grew up here," Damien reasoned. "You must

have walked out there by yourself one day—or did your dad keep you locked up in the house, too?"

"You better check that attitude," Carter warned.

"I'm not gonna get in trouble!" Damien cried.

"That's right!" Carter was shouting now, his patience gone. "Because trouble can't find you in this house! That's it!"

Storming away, Damien slammed the door to his room in fury. Tonya and Carter exchanged looks.

"Kenny," Tonya said slowly, choosing her words with care, "I'm not disagreeing with you...but I think you should listen to him a little more closely."

"I hear everything he says," Carter replied. "I've raised him on my own since he was three—I haven't missed a beat yet."

"I'm not accusing you of missing a beat—"

"He's my son," Carter insisted, "living in my house, so it's—"

"Your rules," Tonya finished for him. She picked up his hand and held it in hers. "I get it. So does he. But I love him, too. I'm as much a mother to him as he's got, whether you like it or not."

"Tonya—"

"We all agree that you should have the final say,"

Tonya went on. "But I think you would be smart to listen to him and listen to me before you make final decisions. That's all." With a sigh, Tonya stood up and walked into the kitchen.

Carter watched her go, knowing that she was right.

★★

"We schooled them Hercules clowns!" Kenyon crowed as he, Junior, Lyle, and Worm strutted down the street, basking in the glow of their victory. None of them even seemed to remember that they were wearing jackets and ties—their game day street clothes. "Junior," Kenyon went on, "you was like Shaq in there—"

"Shaq," Worm said in his official reporter voice, using his tie as a microphone, "you dominated down low tonight, any thoughts?"

"Uhh..." Junior said in his best Shaq imitation, "I dropped a twenty piece and Kobe played his game...We the champions until we ain't the champions anymore."

"We undefeated!" Lyle squawked.

Someone ran up behind Lyle and gave him a shove. "Yo!" Cruz said with a wicked grin. "That was the worst game I've ever seen. I thought it would never end. I was dyin' up there in the bleachers."

"In the bleachers," Lyle said in a bored voice, "while we were handlin' our business on the court."

"One and oh!" Worm put in.

Lyle and Worm knocked hands.

"Hercules is weak." Cruz shrugged. "And you barely beat they ass."

"C'mon dawg," Kenyon said, "don't throw salt—we undefeated."

"That's right," Junior said smugly, "we undefeated."

Junior shoved Cruz playfully, and he broke into a grin. But his wide smile faded as Renny's black Nissan pulled into Hamburger Dan's parking lot and a group of thugs poured out. "Yo," Cruz said quickly, "I'll check you later."

Lyle, Junior, Kenyon, and Worm remembered their jackets and ties with a sudden jolt as they trailed after Cruz, pushing past Renny's thugs on their way to Hamburger Dan's. But Renny didn't even glance in their direction as he shook Cruz's hand and pulled him into a hug.

"I got some paper," Cruz told his cousin as his former teammates streamed into the hamburger joint. He handed Renny a knot of bills wrapped in a rubber band.

Snapping off the rubber band, Renny shuffled through the bills. "Now we're talkin'," Renny said with a smile. "How you livin', Timo? For real, you all right? Here," he said, pulling off a stack of bills, "take some. No, take it."

Reluctantly, Cruz accepted the money. The truth was, he needed it.

"Here's a new bag," Renny said in a low voice as he glanced around quickly. He slipped Cruz a small plastic bag containing a few even smaller bags of crack cocaine. With a quick move, Cruz yanked off his cap, stuck the bag on his head, then pulled his cap over it. He gave his cousin another quick hug, then stood aside as Renny's thugs exchanged gang handshakes.

Cruz cast a quick look at his ex-teammates, hanging out and laughing in the window of Hamburger Dan's, before he disappeared into the dark, quiet street...alone.

★ ★

"Gentlemen," Carter said at Monday's practice, as his players stretched, "let's review the Hercules game."

"Yo," Worm said with a cocky smile, "call out my numbers, sir..."

Carter checked his notebook. "Sir, you had five and four."

Worm frowned. "Sir, I had twelve points and eight assists."

"Five turnovers, four missed free throws," Carter corrected. "We're talking about fundamentals. Until we learn them, we're adding morning practices—every day at six A.M. Mr. Cruz," Carter said, catching sight of the former player near the bleachers, "are you lost, sir?"

Cruz shrugged, trying to look indifferent as he stared at his shoes. "What I gotta do to play?"

"Young man...you do not want to know the answer to that question." Carter turned back to his team. "Gentlemen, as a team, we shot fifty-six percent from the line. Before you leave my gym, each of you will shoot and make fifty free throws."

But the team didn't move. They were riveted to their spots, staring at the immobile Cruz.

After a moment, Carter leafed through his notebook, adding mentally as he went. "Mr. Cruz," he said finally. "You owe me...twenty-five hunded push-ups and one thousand suicides. And they must be completed by Friday."

Cruz walked a few steps away...then dropped to the floor and began doing push-ups.

Carter watched him for a moment, then refocused. "Today, offense," he announced.

The team cheered.

"I have a sister named Linda," Carter began, ignoring the players as they rolled their eyes. "She's smart, she's political, and she's got a big Afro. Linda is our *pick* and *roll*."

"Damn," Kenyon said under his breath. "How many sisters he got?"

The team busted up laughing and Carter gave Kenyon a tight smile. "How many sisters do you think I have?"

"Sir," Kenyon replied, "I count four so far."

"That's right," Carter agreed, "four so far. But I might have a few more. Do you think I would ever lie to you, sir?" There was a twinkle in Carter's eye.

Nobody dared to reply. Instead, they just trotted onto the court and got ready to run their first offensive drill.

★ ★

"Yes, gentlemen!" Carter said, interrupting the offensive set. "You've got to move without the ball, but you've got to be patient on the weak side screen. Set up your man and come off his shoulder hard." Looking at his team, Carter noticed that their attention was trained elsewhere. Turning, he spotted Cruz shaking, struggling to complete another push-up. He hadn't paused since the beginning of practice. Carter walked over to the exhausted Cruz. "C'mon, Mr. Cruz," he said, his voice a low rumble. "Give up. Go home."

Fire burned from Cruz's eyes and his jaw set in a grim line as he cranked out another push-up. But at the last minute, his arms buckled and he collapsed.

Carter walked away. "Switch it up," he called to his team. "Remember I want seven passes before a shot."

As the players began to settle into their offensive play, Cruz walked past and stopped at the baseline. Looking down, he started to run.

"Your assignment is impossible by Friday," Carter told him. "The door is that way."

But Cruz didn't stop running. Each step brought him closer to his jersey.

★★

"It's so early, I can't even get a McMuffin," Lyle

griped as he headed into the gym early the next morning. "How'm I gonna run without a McMuffin?"

Lyle stopped in his tracks and stared in surprise. Cruz was already on the court, running suicides while Carter watched.

"Mr. Cruz, what's your deepest fear?" Carter demanded. "That you are inadequate? When you get scared enough, you can quit and go home."

Cruz was drenched in sweat, but Carter's words only made him run harder.

Giving up, Carter turned to his team and started to drill their fundamentals. First they ran a defensive slide drill, then a three-on-three box-out drill, and then a shooting drill. Finally, Carter led them in a call-and-response drill, so they would remember their plays.

"Some say my sister Cookie is lazy," Carter shouted. "Mr. Stone?"

"Cookie's not lazy, sir!" Kenyon replied. "She just hasn't found her true calling, sir. Until then, she's on unemployment, but she calls it freelance."

"Freelance!" the team shouted.

Carter smiled. "Cookie's our freelance offensive set. Mr. Maddux, who's Ernestine?"

"Ernestine was your prom date in 1972. Sir, I love Ernestine. She can cook, she got that nice big butt. . . ."

"Mr. Maddux!" Carter shouted as the team cracked up.

"Sir," Maddux said with a grin, "she's the stay at home two-three zone. She's the homebody."

"Homebody!" the team echoed.

"Mr. Worm, Linda."

"Linda is your fifth sister, the political one. She don't shave her pits, sir," Worm added, teasing, "it's straight nasty under there."

"Worm!"

"Linda!" Worm shouted. "Big Afro! Pick and roll!"

"Pick and roll!" shouted the team—all except for Worm, who cracked up at something Lyle had said.

"What is funny, Mr. Worm?" Carter demanded.

"Five sisters, sir?"

"I actually have seven sisters, Worm," Carter said smoothly. "You don't believe me?"

Worm shrugged. "I believe you, sir. I was just wondering why yo daddy couldn't give yo mama a night off. Just climb off for one night. Sir."

"Worm, Lyle—twenty suicides!" Carter bellowed. "Now! My mama is a God-fearing woman who sits front row on Sunday." Carter lectured the team as the two boys trudged off to start their run. "Important lesson to learn, all of you: You never speak ill of another man's mama." His voice was stern, but Carter had to hide a smile as he blew his whistle.

There was no doubt—the team was getting it.

CHAPTER 6

It was the end of a long week of practices, and the team was straggling, hanging around the gym. Some of the guys were practicing free throws as the others watched Cruz try to finish up his assignment.

"Mr. Cruz," Carter said, "I'm impressed with your effort, but we've got a game tomorrow, and you came up short—five hundred push-ups and eighty suicides. Please leave my gym." Carter turned to the rest of the team. "Okay, gentlemen, that's it for today. Coat and tie tomorrow." Snapping closed his notebook, Carter started for the door.

Lyle stared dumbly at Cruz, who was standing there, drenched with sweat and drained by his effort. That was it? After everything Cruz had done—after nearly killing himself to join the team—Carter was just going to cut him loose like that? It didn't seem right. Before he even knew what he was doing, Lyle piped up, "I'll do push-ups for him."

Carter turned back, giving Lyle a questioning look.

"You said we were a team," Lyle explained. "One player struggles, we all struggle. One player triumphs, we all triumph."

Carter's eyebrows lifted. He was interested in what Lyle had to say.

"I'll do some...and some suicides, too," Kenyon volunteered.

Lyle had already dropped and started the push-ups, so Kenyon started running. After a moment, Junior had joined Kenyon...and so had Damien. Cruz, exhausted and barely able to walk, limped to the baseline and joined his teammates.

Carter just stood there, watching the boys come together as a team. He wasn't about to do anything to stop it.

★ ★

"Come on," the team shouted as Lyle and Cruz ran the last two suicides together, "this is it! You did it!"

The team exchanged exhausted hand-slaps as

they crossed the baseline. Cruz flopped flat on his back, spent.

"To the baseline!" Carter shouted.

Jumping to the baseline, the team prepared to run.

"*Just* Mr. Cruz!"

The team shuffled away reluctantly as the worn out Cruz struggled to stand at the line.

Carter stepped right up to him. "What's your deepest fear, Mr. Cruz?" Carter bellowed. "Is it your light, not your darkness, that most frightens you?"

Cruz pressed his lips together grimly, preparing for the worst.

Drawing his hands from behind his back, Carter draped a jersey over Cruz's sweaty shoulder. "Welcome to this team, Mr. Cruz."

Taking a deep breath, Cruz held up the Richmond jersey as the players swarmed him. He had earned it. They had earned it—together.

★ ★

It was the middle of the next game, and Richmond was tackling Kennedy—their toughest opponent yet. Damien set a pick and Junior rolled off his man in time to catch Kenyon's pass. With a quick spin, Junior hit the reverse dunk, hanging on the rim a second longer than necessary. Just then, Worm fouled a Kennedy guard—his fifth.

Carter looked at the bench, and spotted Cruz studying the court. "Mr. Cruz!"

Cruz trotted over to the coach. "What is your deepest fear, young man?" Carter asked.

Giving Carter a confused look, Cruz jogged out onto the court to take Worm's place. Lyle gave Maddux a sideways glance. "Why's he keep sayin' that?" Lyle asked. "What's his deepest fear?"

Maddux just shook his head. Nobody understood Coach Carter. The man was a straight-up mystery.

Cruz ran upcourt on offense, grabbed Kenyon's pass, and buried an eighteen-footer. Cruz smiled as he sank the shot. He was back home.

★★

A few weeks later, the Richmond gym was hopping. The place was packed, throbbing with excitement over the big game against Xavier. But one person was not shouting with joy. . . .

"Coach Carter!" Worm's mom shouted from the bleachers. "Why my boy not playin'? Put Worm in the game! Put him in!"

But Carter didn't even glance in her direction. Worm owed him push-ups. He wouldn't play until he had finished them.

At halftime, Richmond was up by six. "Let's start the second half with Diane," Carter said to his team as they clustered around him in the locker room. "Lyle, watch the back door cutter on the weak side. Keep the pressure on..."

A despairing grunt caught Carter's attention, and he turned to see Worm collapse on his last few push-ups. Rolling onto his back, Worm shook his head in frustration.

"Keep your focus," Carter said, turning back to the team. "Keep pushing the ball on every opportunity. On 'Cookie' stay patient. Screeners, seal your man and look for the slip pass. Remember, on the secondary break—"

But Carter didn't get to finish his sentence, because at that moment, Worm's mom burst into the locker room. "Mr. Carter?" she demanded, glaring at the coach.

"Ma'am," Carter said respectfully, "it's the men's locker room."

"Well, ya coulda fooled me," she huffed. "What is this? Why my boy ain't playin'?"

"He owes the team some push-ups," Carter explained. "Team rules."

Worm's mother wheeled on her son. "Jaron?"

"It's my fault," Worm admitted. "I deserved 'em."

Carter nodded at Worm, secretly pleased. But Worm's mama didn't budge. "How many's he got left?"

"About twenty, ma'am."

The heavy woman placed her purse gently on the bench, gathered her voluminous skirt, and knelt onto the locker room floor.

Carter's eyes bulged. "Ma'am—"

"Count 'em off," Worm's mother commanded.

Slowly, painfully, the large woman heaved herself into a push-up. "One..." Carter said.

Worm's mother struggled for number two. "Nineteen," Carter said, cutting the heavyset woman some serious slack.

Dropping to the floor, Worm pressed out the final push-up. "Twenty!" Worm hooted, throwing his arm around his winded mom.

"Mrs. Worm, this young man is lucky to have you," Carter said.

"Damn straight, he is," Worm's mama agreed.

★ ★

"Listen, shorty, I'ma be really real with you," Lyle said to a pretty girl in the empty hallway. "You're my girl, when I'm on the court and the pressure's tough, I think about you, baby girl." The girl's face lit up as Lyle leaned in for a kiss.

"Mr. Lyle," said a voice behind him, "why aren't you in geometry class?"

Lyle looked up to see Coach Carter frowning down at a master schedule. Lyle gulped. "I'm on my way there now, sir," he said quickly, slinging his arm around the girl. "Sir, this is Betty."

"Bella," the girl corrected.

"Bella, sir," Lyle said nervously. "This is Bella." After another moment, Lyle retreated, shuffling off to geometry reluctantly.

Later, as he was walking across the quad, Carter came across Worm, Kenyon, and Cruz helping three girls make banners for the winter dance.

Carter frowned at his players. "I know you all have classes right now. Why aren't you there?"

"Coach," Worm said with a cocky grin, "we're nine and oh. And, well, the teachers let us slide."

"Get to class!" Carter barked. "Now!" The coach

grabbed Kenyon by the elbow as the other two boys scurried away. "I need to talk to you. What are you doin'? I spoke to your guidance counselor, Ms. Callaway."

Kenyon stared at his feet.

"Look at me, sir," Carter commanded. "She showed me your grades. You're carrying a three point three GPA with A's in history and English? And you're out here, cutting class? Kenyon, you've got your whole life ahead of you, and what you make of it is up to you. There is nothing you can't achieve if you want to."

"Well, yeah," Kenyon mumbled, "but..."

"Do you know how smart you are?" Carter demanded. "Sir! Look me in the eye. You've got a serious gift up here." The coach pointed to his head. "And with your ability on the court, colleges will line up to pay for your education. Do you understand this opportunity?"

"Yeah," Kenyon admitted, unable to meet the coach's eye. "But I've got a lot on my mind right now."

"Kenyon, there are people ready to help you with your future—myself and Ms. Calloway." Carter's voice was gentle. "Just tell us how we can help..."

Kenyon looked away. He just couldn't tell the coach about Kyra and the baby. It was too much...

"You all right?" Carter asked.

Kenyon nodded.

"Okay," Carter said finally, "get to class."

★ ★

"Surprise arrival to the poll is Richmond High at nineteenth," Kenyon read aloud from the newspaper as his teammates clustered on the bleachers around him. "The Oilers, having posted a perfect nine and oh mark winning on the road against perennial powerhouses Xavier and Baxter Union...Wait, Junior, you should read this man, they blow you up, kid."

Junior took the paper hesitantly. "Richmond's center has been big," he read slowly, "as the Oilers are boyed...boyed...b—"

"Buoyed!" Carter shouted from behind the team. "Buoyed!"

Junior felt his face burning as he read on. "*Buoyed* by Junior Battle's nineteen-point, eight-rebound-a-night numbers."

"That's my big nigga!" Worm crowed. "He any bigga, he be my bigga nigga!"

"Sit down," Carter commanded as the team

laughed and slapped hands. "Sit down! Nigger is a derogatory term used to insult your ancestors."

Shocked into silence, the team sat, staring at their coach.

"If a white man uses it, you're ready to fight him," Carter went on. "If you use it, you teach him to use it, too. You're saying you don't mind. Well, I mind. So knock it off! Mr. Lyle, what is it that you want out of this basketball season?"

"To win the state championship," Lyle said breezily. The team backed him up, slapping hands.

Carter scowled. "Mr. Lyle, who won the state championship last year?"

"Hell if I know. Sir." Lyle grinned.

"Mr. Lyle, what does your father do for a living?" Carter demanded.

Lyle's smile evaporated. "My father's in jail."

The team fell silent.

"I'm sorry, young man," Carter said finally, "but that doesn't have to be your life. I have four seniors: Battle, Lyle, Kenyon, and Worm. All of whom I believe can play basketball at the college level. College is a realistic option for you, but you must perform in the classroom to have a chance. Have some vision. Where do you see yourself?"

"ESPN," Junior cracked, tossing a basketball into the air and catching it easily.

"Mr. Battle, I spoke to Mr. Gesek today, who told me that he rarely sees you in class," Carter said.

Junior shrugged. "Yeah. We cool, though, me and him. Mr. Gesek is a big basketball fan."

"As of now, you are on suspension," Carter informed him. "You can practice, but you will not play in games until I know from Mr. Gesek that you're caught up in his class."

Junior's eyes bulged in shock.

"Which is a word to the rest of this team," Carter went on. "You signed a contract, you made a commitment. I have your schedules, I will be hearing from your teachers. If you are not performing in the classroom, you will not play. Sit down, Mr. Battle."

Junior slammed the basketball so hard that it bounced against the ceiling.

"Two hundred fifty push-ups, Mr. Battle," Carter said coolly, "you can start now."

"This isn't fair," Junior snapped. "We won those games, not you."

"Five hundred, Mr. Battle. Please sit."

Junior hesitated.

"One thousand!" Carter shouted. "You want to try for two?"

Sneering, Junior spun on his heel and headed for the door.

"Young man," Carter called, after him, "think about the decision you're making by walking out that door."

Junior turned long enough to give Carter a final glare before he slammed out.

CHAPTER 7

Kyra looked up at Kenyon playfully. "I bought us tickets to the dance," she said, holding them up.

But Kenyon didn't smile.

"What is wrong with you?" Kyra demanded.

"Look," Kenyon said as he took Kyra's hand. "I was talkin' to my coach. He thinks I could play ball in college. Straight up."

Kyra shrugged. "Okay. So?"

Kenyon dropped her hand. "So how can I do that and raise a baby?"

"I don't know..." Kyra's voice was defensive. "I'm not sayin' it won't be hard."

"Kyra, it's already hard," Kenyon said firmly. "The kid ain't even here and I'm worryin' about how I'm gonna feed it.... How I'm gonna...everything. *I'm not ready.*"

"So you want out. That's what you're sayin'?"

Kyra's eyes turned hard. "Go ahead," she dared. "*Say it.*"

"If I wanted out, I woulda been out by now, Kyra," Kenyon protested. "I love you. I wanna be with you."

"As long as it's convenient," Kyra added bitterly.

"I'm tryin' to think what's best for both of us."

"This ain't about *us.*" Kyra hissed, shaking her head. "It's about *you. You* don't want me to have a baby. *You* wanna leave Richmond. *You* wanna play college ball. So, you know what? *We* ain't gonna be ready for nothin', okay? *I'm* ready enough to do what I gotta do all by my damn self." She hurled the tickets at him. "Here! Why don't you take yourself to the dance!"

Kyra stormed off, leaving Kenyon standing alone.

★★

"We had another good week," Carter said to his store manager as he sorted through the previous week's receipts.

"Kenny, business is very good," John admitted. "But, I'm on my own, man. You're never here. It gets crazy."

"I know, and I really appreciate—" Carter's sentence was interrupted by the jingle of the bell over the door. "We're closed!" he called without glancing at the door, then turned back to John. "—all the work you're doing. When the season's over—"

A woman hovered hesitantly nearby. Carter turned to look at her.

"Mr. Carter," the woman said, "I'm—"

"Junior Battle's mother," Carter finished for her. "Yes ma'am, I remember you."

"Willa," Mrs. Battle offered. "Willa Battle." She cleared her throat and began. "Mr. Carter, I got a phone call today from a coach at a junior college in Sacramento. They want to see Junior play this Friday."

"Ms. Battle, my rules are simple—"

"And I agree with them," Mrs. Battle said quickly. "I'm not here to argue with your rules, I'm not." Mrs. Battle's voice was soft as she explained, "Almost two years ago now, Junior's older brother, Anton, was killed...and it's been confusing and hard for me and for Junior."

"Ma'am—"

"After you lose a son," Mrs. Battle continued, her eyes welling, "every time the phone rings, your heart stops—"

"Ma'am—"

"I'm not askin' for special attention," Mrs. Battle insisted. "I agree he needs to get straight with his classes, but the idea of junior college had never occurred to my son and...I could move to the Hercules School District, and he could play there—"

Carter shook his head. "Ms. Battle, you need to understa—"

"But I want him to play for you," Mrs. Battle finished.

Carter looked at the proud woman standing before him. He knew that it hadn't been easy for her to come here and talk to him. But he couldn't just dismiss Junior's problems. "Ma'am," he said gently, "as a parent, I can't imagine your loss. And as much as I appreciate your trust in me, I would need to hear it from Junior."

"He's in the car." Mrs. Battle hustled out the door, not waiting for Carter's reply.

A moment later, the bell jingled again, and Junior Battle walked into the sporting goods store, looking sheepish. "I'm sorry for what I said and did at practice," he told Carter, his voice sincere. "And I promise to get caught up with my classes. Sir."

"Young man, you look me in the eye," Carter demanded, and Junior obeyed. "Every part of my body is telling me that this is a mistake," Carter went on, "and that you're gonna make a fool of me."

"No, sir."

Carter hesitated a moment, then said, "You have one thousand push-ups and one thousand suicides before you play. I will see you at practice in the morning."

Junior smiled. He'd never been so happy to get a punishment before in his life.

★★

"But I asked for academic progress reports a month ago," Carter said to Principal Garrison a few days later. He had stopped her in the hall to discuss his players.

Principal Garrison looked at him disbelievingly. "Progress reports? You're the basketball coach."

"Ma'am," Carter growled, "we talked about this. I don't see what the problem is."

"Mr. Carter, do you know what the API is?"

"No, ma'am."

"The Academic Performance Index," Garrison explained. "They judge schools on a scale of one to ten, ten being the best. Do you have any idea where Richmond High scores on that scale?"

"No, ma'am."

"We're a one," Garrison said with disgust, "and have been for the last seven years. The state rewards schools for their performance. Every year I have less money to pay the staff—"

"Ma'am—"

Garrison cut him off. "Can I ask you what it is you want?"

"I want my players to go to college," Carter said simply.

"College?" Garrison scoffed. "Mr. Carter, Richmond graduates fifty percent of our students, a higher percentage of girls, so—in my very educated opinion, if you have fifteen players on your team, you will be lucky to graduate five of them."

"Ma'am, I disagree. I wrote up a contract you should read—"

"Mr. Carter, your job is to win basketball games," Garrison said, her voice low and commanding. "I suggest you keep doing your job."

"Ms. Garrison, your job is to educate these kids by any means necessary," Carter snapped back. "I suggest you *start* doing your job."

★★

Damien split the Xavier defense and shot a rocket to Worm, who lobbed the rock Junior's way. Driving hard to the hoop, Junior slammed in an amazing dunk. The packed gym exploded as the crowd lining the Richmond bleachers leaped to their feet. The buzzer sounded. Final score: Richmond 81, Visitors 64.

A local reporter thrust a microphone at Worm. "They say we nineteenth in the poll," Worm shouted. "Well, I pity anyone on that list—don't rest easy, cause we comin', yo!"

The reporter turned to Cruz. "Timo Cruz, you go five for eight from threeland, and end up with twenty-one points. You guys are twelve and oh—where's this going?"

"I dunno," Cruz said shyly, intimidated by the bright light of the camera, "we just rollin', you know?"

"Where's this goin'?" Lyle demanded, grabbing the mic. Worm and Maddux swarmed in behind him.

"We're goin' to the state championship!" Worm hollered.

"Can I get a yeah?" Maddux demanded. "Can I get a *hell* yeah?"

The crowd went wild. Nobody had any doubts—the Richmond basketball team was unstoppable.

★★

"Gentlemen," Carter said as he addressed his players in the locker room a few moments later, "I just received a call from the director of the Golden Gate Tournament. He invited us to participate in their holiday tournament." The team went crazy, shouting and whistling. Carter held up his hands. "Gentlemen! I also just spoke to Principal Garrison, who assured me that I would receive all progress reports from all of your teachers by the end of the holiday break."

"Sir, our grades are tight, yo," Junior assured him, grinning hugely.

"Sir, not only are our grades fine," Lyle added, knocking hands with Worm, "we're undefeated!"

Carter couldn't help smiling.

★★

The Bay Hill Marching Band struck up a rousing tune as people milled around the immaculate campus. "The third and final day of the twenty-second annual Golden Gate Holiday Tournament finds the host team Bay Hill trying to win the championship against the upstart Richmond Oilers," the announcer reported over the PA system.

In the locker room, Carter addressed his troops. "Gentlemen, you beat two very good basketball teams yesterday. No one expected us to get this far."

"Yeah," Kenyon said, "but now we're playing the team that hasn't lost this tournament in five years. . . ."

"Is it true that we're only here because St. Francis turned them down?" Junior demanded.

Carter looked at him levelly. "There may be teams and fans that don't believe we belong here. I ask you all—" His eyes ran coolly over the players. "—do we belong here?"

Some of the players shrugged. "We belong here," a few of them mumbled.

"What?" Carter demanded. "What is your deepest fear, gentlemen? That you are inadequate?" He let this sink in for a moment, then went on, "They think we're a poor little team from the ghetto. Have some pride in who you are. Where we from?"

"Richmond!" the team shouted.

"Who are we?" Carter demanded.

This time the team roared, "Richmond!"

"Hands in. One, two, three—"

"Richmond!"

Once the players' hands had flown out, Carter reached down and hauled a large cardboard box onto the chair in front of him. "Gentlemen, let's represent my hometown right. I believe you've earned a new look." Opening the box, Carter pulled out a set of brand-new Richmond uniforms—complete with NBA-style tearaway sweats. It was like Christmas morning as the players buzzed around the box, pulling out uniforms and yanking them on.

They were more than ready now.

★★

Lyle and the guard from Bay Hill charged the ball at the same time. But the Bay Hill guard was a fraction of a second faster, and he sent the rock streaking across the court, where a forward grabbed it and scored with a mighty dunk. The Bay Hill crowd went wild, and Carter called his last time-out.

"Listen up," Carter commanded as his players huddled around him at the bench. "We have one minute and twenty left, and we're down by six. We've been here all night. Gentlemen, you've worked hard for this. We can do this." He paused a moment, then roared, "It starts now!" Grabbing his clipboard, Carter slipped into high gear. "Set it up in the one-four and run Candy. Damien's going to hit his three. Lyle, Kenyon: I want a hard screen down there. When he makes it—go Diane—smother them! I want that ball back!"

Carter rose slowly, and the players rose with him as his instructions hit home.

"Oilers on three," Carter said. "One, two, three."

"Oilers!"

When they hit the court, Damien ran Candy, and passed to Worm. Moving quickly, Damien came off a double screen, grabbed the pass and hit his three—boo-yah!

Bay Hill tried to inbound the ball, but the Richmond players were smothering them with defense. The Bay Hill forward shot a bullet pass to the guard, but it just missed, going out of bounds. Now the ball was back with Richmond.

"Hattie Jean!" Carter shouted, holding up his fist to signal the inbound play. "Hattie Jean!"

Shouting over the noise, the players repeated the call. Junior inbounded the ball, and they ran the play perfectly.

Bay Hill ball...but Damien was in there, blocking their shot and tossing a behind-the-back pass to Kenyon. Recovering his balance, Damien raced down the court and caught Kenyon's pass, pulled up, and hit the three before the Bay Hill defenders knew what had happened. Now Richmond was up by two, with twenty-five seconds left on the clock.

Moving quickly, Bay Hill hit a long inbound pass, which beat the Richmond press. Backing it out, the guard set up Bay Hill's offense.

"Here he comes—" Carter shouted from the sidelines. "Weak side help! Lyle, that's you! Rotate!"

Lyle came off his man to cut off the driving Bay Hill Guard, who left his feet and put up a shot, slamming into Lyle as the ball went through the hoop. A whistle screamed, and the ref pointed a blocking foul at Lyle.

"He was there!" Carter screamed in disbelief. "The kid was there! I can't believe you made that call!"

But there was nothing that he could do, except sub in Cruz for Lyle. As the ref walked over to report the foul call, the players lined up for the free throw and Carter yelled for Damien and Kenyon. "Listen," Carter said to the players, "we have nine seconds. Get it in and push it up the court. Kenyon, we're going to you. Run Linda and hit Kenyon coming off the weak side screen." He nodded. "It will be there. Let's go."

A moment later, the Bay Hill guard had hit the free throw, and the Richmond push was on. Damien called the play and Kenyon came off the weak side screen—but a Bay Hill defender knocked Kenyon to the ground.

"Go to the hole!" Carter shouted, realizing his play was a bust. "Go to the hole!"

Driving the lane, Damien put out a hand to ward off the three defenders crowding him. In a fluid move, he left the ground and sank the ball through the hoop.

Carter couldn't hide his grin. David had slain Goliath—his team had won again.

CHAPTER 8

"Tonya, I'm serious," Carter said into his cell phone from his room at the Holiday Inn later that night. "They won the whole thing. Fifteen and oh. Damien was the MVP... Yeah," he said, chuckling, "I'll wake him up. No, hold on, he should tell you." Carter walked down the hall to Damien's room, and knocked softly. No answer. Calling his son's name, Carter walked into the room. But there was nothing but a litter of empty duffel bags.

Damien wasn't there. None of the players were. "Tonya?" Carter said into the phone. "I'll call you back."

★ ★

"D Carter!" Lyle called across the room to Damien. He had just poured a healthy plug of vodka into a bottle of Mountain Dew, which he now flung across the room. But Damien's reflexes were slow—Lyle had been feeding him vodka Dew all night—and the bottle took out an elegant lamp. Damien blinked at his hands, confused, as the other players hooted with laughter. They were having a ball, chillin' with the pretty girls at this fancy suburban party. This was the life.

"Damien," said the girl named Amber who was snuggled tightly against his chest. "Are you drunk?"

Damien shook his head slowly. "I don't drink," he said, slurring his words slightly. He fumbled at the lamp. "Sorry about the...thing."

"It's okay," Amber assured him. She stood up. "Let's go swimming."

"Whoa," Lyle said as Susan—the hostess—led them to a pool and hot tub. "It's December."

"Yeah," Worm agreed, "and my people don't swim."

Susan pushed a button and the solar cover slid off the steaming surface of the pool. "Heated, it's probably ninety degrees."

"We don't have bathing suits," Damien pointed out.

Susan smiled. "Neither do we," she said as she peeled off her top and shimmied out of her jeans. Amber and another girlfriend did the same, and stood before the guys in their bras and underwear.

"You gonna join us?" Amber said. She and the other two jumped into the pool, splashing Lyle and Damien.

Lyle stared at the girls, bug-eyed. "I think I saw this episode of *90210*."

★★

Storming out of the hotel, Carter stood alone, unsure what to do.

Nearby, a cabbie behind the wheel of a minivan lowered his window. "You looking for your team?" he called.

A few moments later, the cab had pulled up in front of the manor. Music was thumping through the walls. Coach Carter walked up to the front of the house, but hesitated at the door. What if his players weren't there? He didn't want to barge in on the wrong party. Carter moved to the window and tried to peep in just as a Mercedes pulled into the driveway and a well-dressed couple stepped out.

"Can I help you?" the man asked warily as he walked toward the house.

"Good evening, sir," Carter said, extending his hand. "My name's Ken Carter, coach of the Richmond Oilers basketball team."

"Richmond?" the man said. "Little lost, aren't ya?"

"Well, sir. I'm looking for my son—"

Just then, a laughing shriek sounded over the music, and the well-dressed man gaped at his house, as though he had just noticed the party going on inside. A moment later, Carter and the man walked through the front door, and stopped dead.

They had just interrupted a game of strip Twister.

The man led Carter to the backyard pool. "You see your son?"

"Damien Carter!" the coach exploded. "Get outta this house! All Richmond players outside!"

Damien scrambled out of the pool and tried to yank on his jeans over his wet boxers as someone turned off the music. A few of the other players skulked out behind him.

It was going to be a long night.

★★

"You should be dreading practice on Monday," Carter announced as the team bus rolled through the rain back toward Richmond. When they had returned to the hotel, the coach had announced that the team had to pack right away—they wouldn't be staying the night, after all. They had lost that privilege...and they were about to lose more. "You think you've run for me before? Leaving in the middle of the night like thieves. I go to your rooms to celebrate, and what do I get? A trek through the suburbs to find my drunken point guard on top of some daddy's daughter."

Worm looked sheepish, but finally, he couldn't resist. "Actually, I was on the bottom."

"Worm, do you want to be on this team?" Carter exploded. "Because you're about six more words away from being gone. Cruz! Open your eyes."

Cruz forced his eyelids up.

Carter scanned the players. "All of you," he said, his voice dripping with disgust. "You think you're big time? Signing autographs? I will ship you all so far down the bench they'll have to pump air to you!"

There was a moment of silence. Then Cruz piped up. "We won the tournament, Coach," he said in a bored voice. "We're undefeated. Isn't that what you wanted? Winners?" He eyed Carter, who didn't reply.

The coach wasn't sure what kind of monster he had created.

★★

Once they reached the school, Carter unlocked

his office and flipped on the light. He had a lot of parents to call. Looking at his desk, Carter spotted two large manila envelopes. Flipping through them, Carter realized what they were—the progress reports he had asked for.

Damien hovered in the doorway.

Feeling his son's gaze, Carter looked up. "Young man, I have no interest in what you have to say."

"Sir? You know I don't drink," Damien said sincerely. "Someone put vodka in my soda. I didn't know—"

"If you're too dumb to figure that out, then you're too dumb to leave the house for a month. You're grounded."

"Sir—" Damien pleaded.

"You wanted me to trust you and let you go out?" Carter demanded. "And this is what happens? You betrayed my trust."

"Dad—"

"Wait for me outside," Carter commanded.

With a frustrated sigh Damien left and Carter turned his attention back to the reports. He scanned the first page, frowning. Quickly, he flipped through the next few pages…finally, he stopped. He placed his palms together and rested his chin on his fingertips for a moment as he digested the results....

Fury simmered through his veins, lighting him up. The progress reports—they were horrible. His players had lied to him. He had trusted them, and they had lied....

Suddenly, his fury overwhelmed him, and Carter exploded. With a clean sweep of his arm, he cleared his desk of everything—the reports, the lamp, paper, pens, stapler—everything went flying. Standing, he threw his chair against the wall in rage.

Finally, with nothing left to throw, he stood at the center of his office, breathing. The team was out of control. He just had to find a way to get through to them.

★ ★

Monday afternoon, Junior and Lyle swaggered down the hallway toward the gym. Cruz, Damien, and Kenyon were already standing there, looking confused.

"What's up, Cruz?" Junior asked. "Big D?"

Cruz stepped aside, revealing a hand-lettered sign. "Practice canceled," the sign read, "Report to the library." A thick chain fastened with a padlock snaked through the door handles. Cruz shrugged.

"Coach givin' us the day off?" The teammates shuffled down the hall to the library.

Carter scanned the players as they took their seats. The coach stood in front of a desk arranged with several neat stacks of paper. Mr. Gesek and two other teachers stood off to the side. Carter waited until the team had settled in, chatting and laughing, and then lashed out. "Quiet, please!" he shouted. Then he held up a pile of papers. "Gentlemen, in this hand, I hold contracts signed by me and signed by you." Carter reached for another tidy stack and held it out. "In this hand, I hold academic reports prepared by your teachers. We have six players failing at least one class, eight players facing 'incompletes' based on attendance. Gentlemen, you have failed—" The coach stopped, then corrected himself. "*We* have failed. We have failed each other. There are a few of you who have honored the contract. Understand that we are a team, and until we all meet the requirements, the gym remains locked."

"But, Coach," Kenyon protested, "I have a three point three."

"That's good, son. Do you score every point for the team, too?" Carter scanned the group of boys.

"You are the Richmond Oilers. Do you know what 'Oilers' stands for? *Only Individuals Learning Everyday Reach Success.*"

A chair squeaked as Cruz stood up, then turned toward the door.

"Sir," Carter called after him, "just know that you're not walking out on me." He motioned to the team. "You're walking out on them."

Pausing, Cruz ran a glance over his teammates. "I had to beg you," he said, his voice a dangerous growl. "Then I ran all those sprints. I did all that." His voice began to rise. "I killed myself for you sir...to get back on this team." Lashing out, Cruz flung a chair across the room. "This is bull!" He didn't say anything more as he stormed out of the library.

There was nothing more to say.

★★

The veins in Principal Garrison's neck bulged as she confronted Coach Carter in his office. "You put a lock on the gym and forced them to meet you in the library?" she demanded. "Are you crazy?"

Carter nodded and leaned forward in his chair. "Ma'am, it's nice to see that you know where my office is."

"Take the lock off that gym," Principal Garrison snapped, letting Carter's comment pass. "My phone has not stopped ringing."

"Maybe someone on the other end of that phone can help us."

"Your intentions are good, Mr. Carter, but your methods are a bit extreme."

Carter met her gaze plainly. "You painted a pretty extreme picture of what these kids face. No one expects them to go to college. No one expects them to graduate."

"So you take away basketball, the one area in their life where they have some success?"

"Yes, ma'am."

"And you challenge them academically?" Principal Garrison added, as though this was the most ridiculous thing she had ever heard.

"Yes, ma'am."

The principal threw up her hands in frustration. "What if they fail?"

"Then *we've* failed."

"Unfortunately," Ms. Garrison growled, "you and I know that for some of these kids, this basketball season will be the highlight of their life."

"Isn't that the problem," Carter asked, "ma'am?"

The principal didn't have an answer for that.

★★

"Coach, this is Worm's uncle, Clarence," said the voice on the answering machine. "I'll get right to the point. You're a dead mother—"

Getting the point, Carter forwarded to the next message. Even though Tonya had warned him not to listen to them, he had already heard a stream of furious messages just like that one.

"I will rip your head off and puke down your throat!" screamed a woman's voice.

Reaching out, Tonya pressed the stop button. "There's a few others on there just like it." She shook her head, half in disbelief, half in admiration. "You put a lock on the gym? You got their attention now, Kenny."

Carter smiled ruefully. "Where's Damien?"

"He's outside. You're doin' the right thing, Kenny," Tonya said as Carter headed toward the door.

Neither one of them moved to answer the phone as it started to ring again.

★★

Damien was already drenched in sweat, having pushed himself through a two-hour workout. His dad could put a lock on the gym, but he couldn't stop Damien from playing in his own backyard. Catching sight of his father at the foul line, Damien tossed him a quick bounce pass. Carter tossed it back, and Damien pushed toward the hoop. Carter blocked the shot easily.

Damien grabbed the ball and Carter started to play tight defense, blocking Damien's next shot, too. Frustrated, Damien started to head off the court.

"Come back here!" Carter commanded.

Damien kept walking.

"Come back here!"

"No, Dad," Damien said, wheeling to face his father. "You win. You always win."

"Damien, I want to tell you something."

"Well, I don't' want to hear it!" Damien cried. "How about that? I got no interest in what you have to say!"

"Damien—"

"You put a lock on the gym so we can't play. You grounded me so I can't leave. What else could you possibly take away from me?"

Carter held his son's gaze. "But you understand what I'm trying to do."

"Oh, I do?" Damien demanded sarcastically.

"How would you know? Have you ever asked me? Conversations with you are one way. You talk, I listen."

"Damien, I need to show you—"

"Going to that party was a big mistake," Damien went on. "I know that. But for once, I was just trying to do what every other guy on the team was doing." Damien didn't understand why his father couldn't get why it was so hard for him to be different from the other guys—to have to obey so many rules.

Carter stood there for a moment, giving his son time to cool off. "Can I show you something?" Carter asked gently. Turning, he led his son into the house.

"I've looked at this a million times," Damien griped as Carter tossed a worn scrapbook in front of him.

Carter frowned. "Well, look again."

Flipping open the book, Damien pointed to a photograph. "Ellis Wood," he recited from memory, "your center—tough, mean." He moved his finger to another picture. "Here's Wynn, right? Mike Wynn—"

"Ask me where he is today," Carter interrupted.

Damien looked up at his father.

"Ellis Wood's in prison," Carter said. "Wynn's okay, married a few times..."

Damien looked back down at the scrapbook. It had always been a relic, an old souvenir of his dad's—he'd never thought of the boys in the photos as people who grew up to be men. Damien flipped through a few more pages until he found the photo he had been looking for. "Johnny Rolen," he said slowly, "your best friend, your point guard, you guys ran the floor."

Carter shook his head. "He's dead. Shot the summer before our senior year."

"Was he in a gang?"

"I guess." Carter shrugged. "But he was just picking his mom up from work. He got out of his car and they shot him, took his keys. His mom watched him die. Great player. Better than me. Good student, too." He reached for the book, but Damien put his hand on it. He wanted to look through it again.

"Do you understand what I'm tryin' to do?" Carter asked.

Damien nodded. For the first time, he really got it.

CHAPTER 9

"In front of you is a complete survey of your academic landscape," Carter announced as he passed out an individual packet to each player. "I have charted a path of improvement for each of you."

"See?" Lyle demanded, pointing to his packet. "I got a two point five. That's good enough."

"All of you can improve," Carter replied, unimpressed by Lyle's average. "Those of you who are under a two point three must improve, and those of you over a two point three, we *challenge* you to improve."

Lyle sighed. "When's this gonna be over, sir?"

"We will not play basketball again until the entire team is at a two point three or better and all of your teachers report that you are current with your assignments," Carter replied.

The players reacted with groans.

"You're all lookin' at me like I just woke you out of a wet dream," Carter told them. "Is that your problem? Am I killin' your fantasy?" Carter began to strut around the room. "I know, you've all got dreams of the NBA—and bein' big ballers with the cars and chains, girls. Livin' the life. I'm not tellin' you not to dream. I'm just tellin' you to have a back-up. Think college." He picked up a book on a nearby table. "Why do I need to know geometry? Think college. Earth science? History? Why? Why do you need to know these things?" he sang, selling the truth like a carnival barker. "Getting good grades in these subjects, combined with basketball talent can get you to college. Why college? If for some strange reason you don't make it to the NBA and you still want to board the train of possibilities …a college degree is your ticket. See the big picture —you want to live 'the life?' College can get you there—the job, the business you want to own, the house, the family, a way to provide for that family…."

He tossed the book in front of Kenyon, who looked up.

"Think college."

★★

"I'm just happy not to be runnin', yo," Worm said a few days later. Lyle, Kenyon, and Damien sat nearby, discussing their fate.

Lyle nodded. "True dat."

"I dunno man," Kenyon said thoughtfully, "he seems for real about all this. Dame, you think he's real on this?"

"Yeah," Damien said, "I think he's dead real." He *knew* his father was dead real.

"He's bluffin'," Lyle announced confidently, "cancelin' practice, okay, but we sixteen and oh! Ain't no way he gonna keep us from playin' against Westminster on Friday."

Damien shrugged. After all, Lyle didn't know his father as well as he did.

★★

The Richmond High School parking lot was packed with TV news vans and satellite trucks. To Coach Carter, it looked as though every news station in the area had staked out Richmond.

"Mr. Carter," called out a field reporter as Carter walked past the locked gym, "is it unfair to the players whose grades qualify them to play?"

"Basketball is a team sport, sir," Carter replied. "We help each other on and off the court."

The reporter turned back to the camera. "Coach Carter has taken the lockout to the next level," he announced. "Richmond was forced to forfeit last night's game. That will be the first loss of the year for the Oilers, and for now, the lock remains on the gym."

"You've got Fremont on Saturday," another reporter said to the coach, "it's the biggest game on your schedule. Richmond would riot if you forfeited the Fremont game."

"Sir, Saturday's far away," Carter replied. "Thank you, I'm off to work."

"Anyone still think Coach is bluffing?" Worm asked as he and the other players watched the media circus.

Lyle eyed Damien. "No offense, D, but I feel like going out there and telling those reporters this is bull."

Kenyon lifted his eyebrows at his friend. "Maybe you shoulda gone to class."

"Maybe you should kiss my ass, Kenyon," Lyle snapped. "My grades are fine. He shoulda locked Junior's dumb ass out."

"Maybe Junior'll knock *your* dumb ass *out*," Junior suggested.

Lyle's eyes narrowed. "Try spelling it first."

Kenyon intervened as Junior lunged toward Lyle. "C'mon, we gotta stay together," Kenyon said. "June, if you need help, I'll tutor you."

Junior scowled. "I don't need help."

"Well, he didn't lock us out for nothing," Kenyon said. "We've all been foolish lately, and all y'all know it."

The truth silenced everyone...except for Worm, who let out a giggle.

Lyle wheeled on him impatiently. "What?"

"Junior," Worm said, "you thought it was bad that we all knew that you failin' science, dawg—now the whole world gonna know!"

Everyone cracked up as Junior ran after Worm.

★ ★

A tight knot of women were waiting for Carter in his office.

"You sonofabitch," Maddux's mother snarled when she saw the coach.

"Ma'am—" Carter began, but another woman cut him off.

"Bethany!" Kenyon's mother shouted. "Let *me* handle this. Mr. Carter...you *selfish* sonofabitch!

You *snake*!" Her eyes shot daggers at Carter. "Don't *ma'am* me, you snake!"

Another woman stepped forward, pushing the other two out of the way. "Remember me?" the large woman demanded, stepping right up into Carter's face. "My son is Worm. And after what he's gone through for your team, that you would lock up that gym…"

"Excuse me, Ms. Worm," Kenyon's mother said, "but you're gonna have to get in line."

Worm's mother lifted her eyebrows. "I don't think so."

The women turned back to the coach, everyone unloading on him at once.

"Ladies!" Carter shouted, holding up a hand. "Ladies!"

The room fell silent.

"I'm more than happy to discuss this with you," Carter said calmly, "but please. Let's step into the hallway. Let's be grown-ups about this."

The women eyed each other doubtfully as Carter motioned toward the hall. After a moment, they filed out. Carter stood at the door, politely waiting for them to pass.

Once all of the women were outside his office, Carter spun around, shut the door, and locked it.

The muffled shouts and pounding on the door didn't even bother him as he went to sit down at his desk.

★ ★

"Young men," Carter said in the library later that afternoon, "it's been a long day. All the reporters, cameras..." He shook his head, not even bothering to mention the angry mob of parents that had met him at his office or the fact that someone had busted out the windows of his store. "Let's take this opportunity to say anything you need to say while that door is closed. This is about us."

"Bull," Junior griped. "This ain't about us, this is all about Coach Carter."

"We're a basketball team," Lyle piped up, "and all I see is you on TV, gettin' famous, eatin' that stuff up."

"That's all you see?" Carter demanded.

The players grumbled in agreement. "That's what I see," one of them mumbled.

"I see a system that is designed for you to fail!" Carter exploded. "You're so fixed on your stats, I'll give you some. This school only graduates fifty percent of its students. Half of this school is not graduating. Only six percent of Richmond students go on to college. Which tells me that when I'm walking down the hall looking into your classes, maybe one student in that entire class will go to college." Carter paced the front of the library like a caged lion. "Gee, Mr. Carter, if I don't go to college, where I'm goin'? Great question. Here's the answer for the young African-American men in here—you're probably going to prison."

The players stared at the coach in shock. None of them had any idea where this was coming from.

"In this county thirty-three percent of black men between the ages of eighteen and twenty-four will be arrested," Carter went on, ticking off the stats on his fingers. "One in three. Look at the guy on your left, now the guy on your right—one of you is getting arrested. Research tells us that seven out of ten African Americans have been or are in jail or prison. Growing up in Richmond, you are eighty percent more likely to go to prison than go to college!"

Carter let the silence that had fallen over the room do the talking for him. He knew that the truth was hard to hear. "That's tough math, gentlemen," he said finally, his voice gentler now. "Go home tonight and take a look at your life, at your parents' lives. Ask yourself, do you want better? If the answer is yes, I'll see you back here tomorrow. I promise to do everything I can to get you to college, to get you a better life."

Carter nodded at his players and walked out. He only hoped that some of them had heard him.

★★

Coach White caught up with Carter in the parking lot. "Kenny," White said, shaking his head. "You've really whacked the hornets' nest with a stick."

Carter laughed, exhausted. "I guess the nest needed a whack."

White smiled, looking off into the distance thoughtfully. "Probably so," he admitted, "probably so. Kenny," he went on, changing gears, "no one's sure what you're doin' is legal, and the school board's having a meeting to determine if it is. Friday at five. You need to be there."

Carter looked his old mentor in the eye. "I'll be there," he promised.

Coach White walked away, and Carter turned to find his car. He didn't have any trouble spotting it.

Someone had dumped garbage all over it.

★★

Carter tossed a newspaper onto the kitchen table, knocking a cup to the floor. He'd just finished reading another angry editorial calling for his resignation. Rage boiled in his chest as he paced the kitchen floor. "I almost took the lock off that gym today," Carter confessed to Tonya. "I had the key in my hand. I should just end this whole thing."

"Kenny Carter," Tonya said, "you need to sleep."

"I'm tryin' to help people who don't want help," Carter went on. "For what? I got a store with boards for windows, people spittin' on me, I haven't slept in two days."

"You're gonna see this through." Tonya's voice was firm. "So sit down before I knock you down."

Carter looked at her and smiled weakly before collapsing in a chair.

★★

"Yo, it's Allen Iverson," Renny howled as Cruz walked up to him. They shook hands and hugged. "What's up, cuz?" Renny asked, looking carefully at Cruz. Renny frowned, thinking that his cousin didn't look well. "Where you been? Ain't nobody seen you, man. I was gettin' nervous for a minute.

You been on some solo creep?"

Cruz shrugged listlessly. "Yeah."

"How's biz wit you, man?" Renny asked, punching Cruz in the shoulder. "You got some paper for me?"

Reaching into his pocket, Cruz pulled out a ratty roll of bills and a baggie containing smaller baggies of unsold crack rocks and handed them over.

"Yo," Renny said. "What's with the product?"

"I don't know, man," Cruz said vaguely. "I've just been walkin' around. I ain't been hustlin' too much."

Renny's voice took on a faint edge as he said, "Well, I need you to hustle a little harder, then."

"Take this, too," Cruz said, pulling a gun out of his waistband.

"Whoa! Whoa! Whoa!" Renny cried, leaning hard on his cousin. "What's with this? Where you goin'?"

"Don't push me, Renny!" Cruz warned, glowering. "I'm tryin' to sort this stuff out. I don't know what I'm doin' right now. I just think I gotta get out of the game for a minute."

Renny backed down a little, nodding. "You gotta get your head straight."

Cruz softened. "You one of the only people in my life ever helped me."

"You damn straight!" Renny agreed. "When your mom lost her apartment and you didn't have no place—I took you in. I hooked you up." Renny looked at his cousin closely, searching his face. "You got that coach in your head. You think that coach really tryin' to help you? Listen, Timo, we family," he said gently. "You gotta look out for yourself. Hear me? We gotta stay together. I got your back, but you can't disappear on me. All right? All right?"

Cruz nodded, and the cousins shook hands and hugged.

"All right." Renny handed back the gun, and Cruz tucked it into place along his waistband. "But keep this for now. And take all this back," he added, handing both the money and the crack to Cruz, "and let's go move some. I gotta head back to Division, roll with me. We'll just kick it for a bit."

Cruz nodded. "All right," he said finally. "Cool."

The two piled into Renny's Nissan Maxima and took off to a nearby liquor store, where someone was waiting for Renny. "What's up, dawg?" Renny asked the guy as he got out of his car. "Yo," he called to his cousin, "I'ma get a drink, Timo. You want something?"

Cruz just shook his head as he looked across the street, where he spotted Kenyon, Junior, Worm, and Lyle at the Corner Store Restaurant. Lyle and Worm were clearly scamming on a couple of girls—and they hadn't yet noticed the three guys who were walking up to them. Cruz thought he recognized them—they were from the nearby rival school, Pinole. Whatever was going down, it didn't look good.

Trotting across the street, Cruz walked in on an argument.

"C'mon Worm," Junior begged his furious-looking teammate, who was facing off with one of the Pinole guys, "let's go. Let it alone."

Everyone in the restaurant was standing. They had cleared away from the fight that was clearly about to take place.

"We're good to go," the guy challenged.

"Oh, you good to go?" Lyle screamed, looking half-crazy with fury. "You good to go? Let's go! Let's go!" Reaching out, Lyle grabbed the Pinole guy's jacket, and whirled him around. Both sides moved to join the fight. Cruz reached for his gun just as Junior and Worm pulled Lyle off the guy.

Before anything could happen that they would

be paying for for the rest of their lives, the Richmond players hustled Lyle outside and into the street. The Pinole guys piled into their car and drove away.

"All right," Worm said to Lyle, breathing deeply. "All right. It's cool."

Lyle yanked away from Junior and Worm, taking a moment to collect himself.

Grinning, Cruz shoved Lyle. "Nice to see the fight in you, dawg," Cruz teased. "I'll see you later." With a nod, Cruz trotted back across the street, where Renny was waiting for him.

Just then, the guy who had been waiting for Renny in the liquor store parking lot pulled his gun. Time seemed to slow down as Cruz watched the guy pull the trigger...watched his cousin crumple to the ground.

The young man got into his car and drove away, but Cruz didn't even try to stop him. He was only thinking of Renny. Cradling his cousin in his arms, he tried to help Renny sit up.

"Call nine one one!" Worm screamed as he and the other players poured into the parking lot. "Call nine one one!"

But it was already too late.

CHAPTER 10

Carter walked warily to the front door, where someone was pounding frantically, ringing the bell at the same time. When he yanked open the door, he saw Cruz standing there, his eyes wild.

"I wanna come back," Cruz said in a desperate voice.

"Son, what's goin' on?" Carter asked as he flipped on the porch light. He took a step toward Cruz, who backed away. "What happened?"

"Renny, he…he…" Cruz squeezed shut his eyes. He couldn't get the image out of his mind, he couldn't get the words past his lips. "They shot him," he said finally. "They shot Renny."

Carter took another step toward Cruz, who had backed to the edge of the porch. Part of Carter feared that Cruz would bolt—that, whatever had happened, Cruz would leave before they had a chance to make it right.

"What I gotta do to play?" Cruz asked.

"Cruz," Carter said as Damien appeared like a silent ghost in the hall, "why don't you come inside?"

"You gotta let me back," Cruz begged. "What I gotta do to get back?"

By now, Carter could see the blood on Cruz's shirt. "Son, c'mon inside now." Carter took another step toward the boy, and this time Cruz didn't back away.

"I'll do it. Push-ups—I'll do it right now. Running, I don't care." His eyes started to fill with tears. Cruz knew one thing: he had to get back on the team. He needed to be on the team. "You gotta take me back, sir. Please, sir."

"Okay, young man," Carter said gently. "We got you back. You're back with us now, okay?"

Reaching for Cruz, Carter pulled him into a hug. Cruz clung to him as though his life depended on it.

★ ★

There had never been a more packed or rowdy meeting of the Board of Education. Teachers, students, and irate parents had come to discuss the situation at Richmond High. The seven-member board sat on a dais, listening to arguments on both sides.

The president of the Board of Education peered down at Coach Carter. "The state only requires a two point oh GPA for participation in extracurricular activities?"

Carter nodded. "Yes, ma'am."

"And according to your contract," President Martinez went on, "the players agreed to maintain a two point three?"

"Yes ma'am, among other things."

"Other things like...?" Ms. Martinez prompted.

"Ma'am, like attending all classes," Carter replied, "sitting in the front row of all classes, a dress code on game days."

Ms. Martinez pursed her lips thoughtfully. "I see. Mr. Carter, does the lockout include practices *and* games? And do you have a set time period?"

"There will be no basketball," Carter said firmly, "no practices, no games until we as a team meet our academic goals."

An angry murmur simmered through the room.

"Okay," Ms. Martinez said. "In the interest of time, I will open the floor to comments."

A teacher whom Carter recognized from the Richmond science department stood up. "As a teacher," the man said, "I was offended when asked by a coach to produce progress reports. Nowhere in my contract does it say that I have to do so. It creates more work. This lockout has brought negative media attention that questions our abilities as educators. Mr. Carter has overstepped his bounds. End this madness. End this lockout."

The room erupted into cheers. Just then, Junior, Damien, Kenyon, and Lyle slipped into the rear of the room. They had been told not to come, but they refused to stay home—they had to know their future.

Another man stood up. "I'm Jason Lyle's uncle," he said, "and that boy lives to play ball. He comes to school every day now. If he doesn't have basketball, God knows what he'd be into."

"This morning, he canceled the Fremont game!" Worm's mom bellowed, jumping to her feet. "That's the biggest game of the year! I got scouts comin' to see my son play. These boys are sixteen and oh. This whole school, this whole community is behind this team. Everybody comes to every game. Basketball is the only thing these kids got, and you gonna let Carter take it away from them? Unh-unh. Not gonna happen."

The room rang with shouts of agreement as Worm's mother sat back down.

"Yes, I'd like to make a motion," said a member of the board.

"Great, Mr. Walters," President Martinez said.

"I move that we remove Mr. Carter as head basketball coach," said Mr. Walters, and the room chorused their agreement. Carter stared at Mr. Walters in shock as a few team parents leaped to their feet to second the motion.

"This board does not have the authority to terminate employment of a staff position," Martinez explained.

The Richmond science teacher stood up. "I move to end the lockout and let the kids play."

"I second!" someone shouted.

"I third!" called someone else.

Martinez nodded. "Okay, the motion passes. We will vote to end the basketball lockout."

Carter hauled himself to his feet and addressed the board members. "I ask you to consider the message that you're sending these kids," he said, struggling to control his voice. "The same message that we as a culture send to pro athletes, which is that they are above the law. I'm trying to teach them a discipline that will inform their lives, give them choices. If we teach them now at seventeen that they don't have to obey rules, you tell me how long it is before they're out there breaking laws. I played basketball at Richmond thirty years ago. It was the same then. Many of my teammates went to prison. A few are dead. This is a very special group of kids. I came here with the desire to make a change for a few of these boys. This is the only way I know how to do that. If you vote to end the lockout, I promise you," turning, he glared at the gallery of parents and faculty behind him, "—you will not have to terminate me—I will quit."

For the first time, the room fell quiet.

Damien, Lyle, Junior, and Worm exchanged looks. Quit? It had never occurred to them that they might lose their coach over this.

"Thank you, Mr. Carter," Ms. Martinez said. "The board now recognizes seven voting members. I put to those members a vote to end the lockout. Those in favor of ending the lockout will raise their right hand when called upon. I will vote first by not raising my hand."

Carter nodded at her, grateful for the support.

"Principal Garrison?" Ms. Martinez called.

The principal left her hand down, and Carter's heart leaped. He knew that she didn't agree with him, but he was glad that she was backing him up.

"Phil Walters," Ms. Martinez said, and the man raised his hand.

"Benson Chiu?" Mr. Chiu also raised his hand.

President Martinez looked at the next board member. "Valerie Walker?"

She raised her hand.

Ms. Martinez nodded. "Our parent reps. Mr. Cepeda?"

His hand went up.

"And Ms. Nyugen?"

The room exploded as the final hand went up.

"The lockout ends by a vote of five to two," President Martinez announced.

Rising, Carter turned and walked out. He would hand in his resignation in the morning.

★ ★

The Richmond players sat slumped in a booth a Hamburger Dan's, still numb from what they had witnessed at the school board meeting.

"You don't get it," Kenyon said, his eyes flashing dangerously. "He quit! He's done!"

"We'll coach ourselves," Junior put in.

Lyle stared glumly at his fries. "I can't believe they voted him out."

"Well, whatever," Worm said lightly. "We get to play."

Kenyon's fury hit a flash point. "It's not about us!" he exploded. "Don't you get it? It's over, man. It's *over*. He was tryin' to help us and we messed it up." He stormed away, leaving his teammates staring after him.

And the absolute worst part was that they knew he was right.

★★

Principal Garrison stood by Carter's black Mercedes as he pulled an empty box from the trunk and looked over at the gym. She knew he was about to tell the players that he was leaving, and she didn't want him to go. "Mr. Carter?" Principal Garrison said. "Are you sure you want to do this? I know we haven't always seen eye to eye, but you've done such a great job with these boys, it seems wrong to just—"

Carter's voice was grim. "Ma'am, no offense, but all the work I did with those boys was negated by ending the lockout."

Principal Garrison was looking at the box as though she hoped it would disappear. "I don't think that's true—"

Carter looked her in the eye. "The board sent the message loud and clear: winning high school basketball games is more important than graduating from high school and going to college." The coach shook his head sadly. "I'm sorry, I can't support that message." With that, he forced himself to walk toward the school.

Reaching the gym, Carter saw that someone had already cut the chain from the door. It lay on the ground nearby—tossed aside. Sighing in disgust, Carter stooped to collect the chain, and placed it in his box. That was it—the sign that he was doing the right thing. Things were never going to change—he'd been a fool to think so. Completely resigned, he shoved open the door and stopped, staring at what he saw there.

The gym was lined with rows of desks, and in each desk was a Richmond player...studying. For the first time in his life, Carter stood speechless.

Lyle looked up from his book. "Sir, they can cut the chain off the door, but they can't make us play."

Damien smiled at his father. "We decided we're gonna finish what you started, sir."

Carter's throat was thick with tears—he couldn't speak. Carter was a man who'd had many proud moments...but this was the proudest of his life.

"Yeah," Worm chirped, lightening the mood, "so leave us be. We got work to do. Sir." With an indifferent shrug, Worm looked back down at his book. After a moment, a look of understanding began to dawn across his face. "X equals nine?" he said aloud, peering over at Lyle, who had been helping him. "Am I right? X equals..." Worm jumped up in excitement. "I can do this, man! I got it! Gimme some love!"

The other players jumped up to give him high-fives.

Smiling, Carter turned toward the exit as the players settled back down to their studies. Suddenly, a lone voice rang through the gym.

"Our deepest fear is not that we are inadequate."

Turning, Carter saw Cruz standing by a desk. "Our deepest fear," he recited, "is that we are powerful beyond measure. It is our light, not our darkness, that most frightens us."

Carter blinked. "Written by—"

"Marianne Williamson," Cruz replied. "And sir, I just want to say..." Cruz swallowed hard, blinking hard to fight back the tears that threatened to overwhelm him. "Thank you. You saved my life."

Beaming, Carter turned to leave the gym. He knew now that no matter what happened—no matter whether Richmond won or lost the rest of their games, even if the team never played again—they had won.

★★

A week later, Carter blasted into the library where his team was studying. "I can't believe these reports," he shouted, slamming a thick manila envelope onto a table. "It's unbelievable. Junior? Worm?" He glared at the players, who exchanged worried looks. "Look, I know you've been tryin', but..." Shaking his head, a slow smile spread across Carter's face. "Now you've succeeded. Each of you, every last one of you, has reached your goal. Gentlemen, let's play ball."

The team blew up—cheering, hugging, and slapping hands as though they had just won a championship game.

Carter shook hands with Mr. Gesek and Mrs. Sherman, who had donated their time to help the players, and had been tutoring them for weeks. It had finally paid off.

★★

By the next morning, the entire school—the entire city—knew that the Richmond v. Arlington game was on. As Carter parked his car and headed toward the school, he was thronged by reporters.

"So you play Arlington tomorrow night?" a reporter demanded. "With no practice for two weeks? What's the plan?"

A smile played at the corners of Carter's mouth. "Sir, we plan to stretch real well."

"Coach," another reporter said, "the lockout got so much media attention—you were on CBS, CNN, and NBC—did part of you think that this might happen? I mean, was this all some master plan?"

Carter stopped in his tracks. "As I think about what you just said, that this lockout got so much attention...it reminds me that I'm a basketball coach. Thank you all." With that, he nodded at the reporters and disappeared inside the school.

CHAPTER 11

At the opening tip, Junior went airborne, finding Cruz, who shot a bullet to Worm. A quick no-look to Junior, and the ball was through the hoop with a massive dunk. The crowd roared. Richmond was back!

By the end of the fourth quarter, Richmond was up by eleven. It was a total rout, but the players wouldn't stop—they were having too much fun. The ball swung out to Kenyon, who pulled up and went for the three. *Swish!* All net.

The stands were in chaos as the Richmond fans stomped and cheered. Damien had the ball, and dribbled out the last few seconds. "Three!" the fans chanted as the clock ticked down. "Two! One!"

The buzzer sounded. It was over. Final score: Richmond 82, Visitors 68.

The players slapped hands, hugging and cheering.

It felt good to be back.

Looking up into the stands, Kenyon spotted Kyra making her way down toward the court. Her warm brown eyes locked onto his as she walked up to him. "Nice game, Kenyon," she said.

He smiled, feeling a familiar dull ache in his heart. He missed her. But he didn't know how to tell her that. He didn't know what to do about the baby—about anything. "Thanks," was all he managed to say before the fans stormed the court, and a human tidal wave swept Kyra aside, pulling her out of sight.

★★

Carter's office was packed with players. The air was thick with tension and the heat of bodies. Coach White stood beside Carter as everyone stared at the phone, willing it to ring.

The Oilers had won another game, beating Kennedy...again. And now there was a chance that they would be invited to the state tournament....

"We forfeited two games in the lockout," White said nervously. "So we lost our top seeding in the playoffs."

The phone rang. The silence was absolute as Carter reached for the receiver.

"Coach Carter, how may I help you?"

The players stared at the coach's face, searching for some clue as to what was being said on the other end of the line. But, as usual, Carter's face was impossible to read as he said, "Yes, sir. Yes, sir, we understand that. I see. Well, sir…we accept."

The team went crazy, letting out a deafening cheer as Carter hung up the phone. He smiled, waiting for the excited players to quiet down.

"We are a low seed in our bracket, so we will travel," he explained.

"Sir, where we goin'?" Lyle asked, grinning. "Who'd we get?"

"St. Francis."

The players fell silent at the memory of their humiliating preseason defeat at the hands of Ty Crane and the rest of the St. Francis crew. Junior pushed his way out of the room, and Damien followed him with his eyes, dread forming a knot in the pit of his stomach.

Nobody wanted to face St. Francis.

★★

Kenyon toyed with the small plastic bag in his hand as he pressed the buzzer to Kyra's apartment. A tired-looking young woman with two small children stepped out of the building. Kenyon recognized her as Kyra's cousin. In the next moment, Kyra walked out and helped her cousin get the children down the steps.

Kyra hugged her cousin warmly before watching her walk away with her two children in tow.

Kenyon watched her nervously. He hadn't spoken to her since the game. "How you been?" he asked, his voice tentative.

Kyra nodded. "I'm good."

"You look good."

"Thanks," Kyra said. "So do you. Considering."

"Yeah." Kenyon shrugged. "Life's been a little crazy with the lockout and everything."

"It'll work out."

"For sure." Kenyon gestured toward the steps. "Listen. Sit down a minute." Kyra took a seat on the steps, and Kenyon sat down close to her. "You know," Kenyon said, his heart thumping wildly, "I been trying to get my head straight about ...things. A lot of things. Especially us."

Kyra looked at the ground. "Kennie..."

"Kyra. Just listen," Kenyon begged. "Please."

Kyra leaned back and looked at him, listening.

Kenyon cleared his throat and started again.

"For a long time, there was just my Mom, my boys, and you. That's what I counted on. Now I'm tryin' to count on myself. I'm doin' all right, but without you, nothin' good feels as good. It's like some happy part of me is missing."

A thrill shot through Kenyon as Kyra reached over and stroked his cheek. He gazed into her eyes for a moment, then reached into his bag. "I got something for you. And it ain't from the ninety-nine cent store."

Kyra gasped as Kenyon held up a T-shirt. Sacramento State was emblazoned across the front. "They gave you a scholarship?" she squealed, her eyes wide.

Kenyon grinned from ear to ear. "Full ride."

"That's great, Kenyon! I know you're gonna blow up there."

"*We're* gonna blow up," Kenyon corrected, taking Kyra's hand. "I told them about you, the baby. They're gonna help us."

Kyra was silent for a moment. "Kenyon," she said finally, "there is no baby. I decided not to go through with it."

"Kyra..."

"I had a choice to make, and I made it. I did it

for me, Kennie." Her eyes welled with tears.

"Why didn't you tell me?" Kenyon asked. "I would've gone with you. I'm sorry, baby. I'm sorry you had to go through that by yourself."

"My mom went with me," Kyra said gently.

Kenyon pulled her into his arms, holding her close. "You should go to school and play ball..." Kyra said. "Become everything you can be. I want that for you because that's what's real. That's what you should be about now, Kennie."

Kenyon looked at Kyra. He couldn't believe that she was so strong. "I want you to come with me," he told her after a moment. "I love you, Kyra. I want you to come with me."

The tears in Kyra's eyes lit up like diamonds in the fading light as she smiled at him. "Straight up?"

"Straight up, baby."

"Maybe I could take some classes," Kyra said quickly. "Do they have a teaching program? I'd make a good teacher. Don't you think I'd make a good teacher?"

Kenyon lifted his eyebrows. "The way you tell everybody what to do? Oh, yeah. For sure."

Kyra swatted him playfully, and Kenyon wrapped her in an even tighter hug. He knew that—whatever was going to happen—they would get through it together.

★ ★

"Ty Crane," Bill Walton said into the microphone as he looked up at the towering form of the St. Francis player, "you average thirty-two points and thirteen rebounds a game, All-American, amazing. Tonight, you and St. Francis start your bid to defend your state title. What kind of threat is Richmond?"

Crane's face betrayed no emotion as he looked directly into the camera. "No threat. I promise you. None."

Bill Walton continued his commentary as Coach Carter entered the enormous San Francisco State University arena, followed by all seven of his sisters. The crowd's energy was intense—it seemed as though half of California had turned out to watch this game.

"St. Francis is one of the best high school teams in the nation, with Ty Crane believed to be a shoo-in for the NBA draft pick next year," Walton said into the camera. "On the other side of the court is Richmond, a team that's had a media-worthy season as well. Sixteen and oh and then locked out of their gym. If my research serves, Richmond High School has never played in a state tournament game, but they actually met up with St. Francis in a preseason game where they were losing by forty points before forfeiting after three quarters. Let's hope tonight they can last the whole game."

Junior eyed Crane as he walked onto the court. Junior found Crane's confidence infuriating—he didn't even respect the Richmond players. All Junior wanted to do was teach Ty Crane a lesson. He hoped he'd have a chance.

From the very first tip, Junior leaped into action, slamming the ball toward Damien, who had to wrestle it away from a St. Francis guard. Setting up the half-court offense, Damien brought the ball upcourt. Richmond passed a few times, and finally the ball found Kenyon, who dove into a small opening and hit a twelve-footer. The Richmond crowd went wild.

Damien set up Delilah, the full-court trap defense, as St. Francis moved the ball quickly upcourt. Junior settled over Crane, giving him heavy pressure. But St. Francis moved the ball around the perimeter. Worm tried to work the D on his man, but the guard pulled up and sank the nineteen-footer.

By the second quarter, things were looking grim for Richmond. Junior was still guarding Crane like Fort Knox. But it was no use. Crane grabbed the ball and shot a twelve-foot fadeaway. St. Francis 16, Richmond 8.

The ball went to Junior on the blocks. Crane bit on Junior's shoulder fake, and Junior went up and under, getting the easy layup.

Third quarter, and Carter was starting to work up a sweat on the sidelines. At the last moment, the St. Francis forward found Crane under the basket, and he layed it in for an easy two. "Box out!" Carter shouted from the sidelines. "Watch the weak side boards."

Worm laid out a pretty back-door pass to Kenyon, who tossed in the layup. But St. Francis didn't give up. In the next play, a cocky guard waved off the pick and got by Worm with a killer crossover. The St. Francis guard hit his shot, just as Worm fouled him.

The St. Francis bench broke into cheers as the whistle blew. Worm slammed the ball against the court in frustration. It was the third quarter, and the score was St. Francis 36, Richmond 21.

Carter called a time-out, and his team clustered around him. "Gentlemen, you told me you belonged," the coach said. "You're playing like you don't. All year long, we've played our games. Right now, we're playing theirs. When we step out there, we take it to the next level. We're going to run, we're going to pressure the ball, we're going to play with confidence. We're going to be the Richmond Oilers!"

The players looked at one another. The coach was right. They'd let St. Francis defeat them in their minds. They had to get back into the game.

"All right," Carter said, "we're in Diane. Worm, you can hold this kid. Force him left, and when he crosses over, jump him. Damien, push the tempo. Lyle and Kenyon, crash the boards. Cruz, spot up in transition. Junior, you continue to shut this kid down—we'll be there in the end. Who are we?"

"Richmond!"

It was the final quarter, and Richmond had finally started playing like they were born to play ball. Junior made a monster dunk, and grabbed the rebound. He passed to Worm, who came off the screen and found Lyle, who drove in strong. Crane came in late, fouling him, and Richmond huddled up at the foul line.

"Mr. Cruz, get Kenyon," Carter said, subbing in Cruz. "After he makes this, go Delilah. Keep the pressure on!"

After the foul shot, Damien drove the baseline, drawing a double-team as he took flight. The rock found Cruz in the corner, and he nailed the shot.

A few moments later, Damien hit a gorgeous three-pointer. Then Junior stripped the ball away from Crane. As Crane griped to the ref, Kenyon took the ball and sent it upcourt to Worm, who spun off of his defender and hit the shot.

With twenty-six seconds left to play, Crane made an easy break-away as Junior hustled to recover. Crane went in for the dunk, but Junior got a piece of it, and both players fell to the ground in a heap. Crane shouted for the foul, but the ref shook his head. All business, Junior started to head upcourt as Crane exploded in rage, shoving Junior. The teams were starting to get physical as Carter called his last time out, leading his players to the bench. The St. Francis players seemed rattled as they looked to their coach.

"We got 'em," Carter told his players calmly.

"Nobody's taken them to the wire all year. Now it comes down to character. I've just seen theirs, and I know yours." The coach grabbed his clipboard. "We're going to run Candy. Spread the floor." He looked at Worm. "Worm, you gotta sell the pass to Damien. Junior, we're going to you on the weak side steal. Gentlemen, just because we deserve it, doesn't mean they're going to give it to us. Leave everything on this court. Who are we? One, two, three—"

"Richmond!"

Bringing the ball upcourt, St. Francis bought Worm's terrific fake to Damien. There was just enough room for Junior to take the ball off the screen, and he hit a jump hook. The Richmond fans went crazy—they were up by one with four seconds left.

A St. Francis player heaved the ball downcourt, and Crane caught it on the run. Junior was closing in as Crane went in for the twenty-five footer. The buzzer sounded just as the ball sailed through the hoop.

The Richmond Oilers collapsed to the ground in disbelief. They had lost. Junior stood gaping at the scoreboard. It just didn't seem possible.

Feeling a pair of eyes on him, Junior turned to see Ty Crane standing beside him.

"Nice game, man," Crane said, giving Junior a quick hug.

Pride shot through Junior, who drifted away as Bill Walton hurried over to interview Crane. "Ty Crane, as predicted, a victory. But you were held to eleven points by Junior Battle, who had nine blocks in the contest—"

Carter walked over to shake the hand of the St. Francis coach. "Good luck, Mike. Nice game, sir."

"Coach, it's great what you did with these kids," he told Carter warmly. "I mean it. Fantastic."

"Thank you, sir," Carter said. "Thank you, sir." Just then, Carter caught sight of Damien, who was fighting back tears. Carter put his arm around his son, who buried his face in his father's shoulder. "I'm very proud of you, son," Carter whispered in Damien's ear. "I love you. You played a great game. You hear me?"

Damien nodded, and tried to force a smile. Carter hugged him again, and the two men headed toward the locker room.

It was stone quiet as the players sat on the benches, dejected. Carter banged a locker, saying,

"Well . . ." He pressed his lips together, then added, "That sucked."

The players smiled sadly.

"Damn good shot, though," Carter said. "Mr. Cruz, sir. Would you trade what we achieved this year for a few more points on that scoreboard?"

Cruz looked his coach straight in the eye. "Hell, yes."

Laughter rippled through the team as Carter smiled.

"Me, neither," said the coach. "Tonight, I felt something better than winning. Some may say we lost a game tonight, but I say without flinching that we didn't lose tonight, the clock just ran out. You did tonight what champions do. You never gave up. And champions don't hang their heads."

Cruz gazed at Carter and nodded. The other players looked at each other, realizing that the coach was right.

"What you've achieved goes far beyond the crossover dribble," the coach went on, "the three-point jumper, or the trap defense. What you achieved some men never achieve. What you've achieved is the ever-so-elusive victory within. You have made me proud. Four months ago, I took this job, and I had a plan. Well, that plan failed. I came to teach players and you became students. I came to coach boys, and you became men. And if they walked in here right now and gave me my choice of all the teams in California to coach, you know which one I'd choose?"

Kenyon and Worm looked at each other. "Richmond?" they guessed, hesitantly.

Carter held his hand to his ear. "Rich what?"

"Richmond!" Cruz shouted.

Carter grinned. "Rich what?"

"Richmond!" the team cried, and the locker room rang with their shouts as the players leaped to their feet, hugging and high-fiving. They were proud...and they had every right to be.

EPILOGUE

The Richmond Oilers did not win the state championship...but they won nine college scholarships.

Junior Battle went to UNLV on a full scholarship.

Timo Cruz attended Tulane University and returned to California to become the starting quarterback for Humboldt State University.

Kenyon Stone attends San Jose State University and is currently considered a lock for the NFL draft.

Damien Carter continued to dominate the league as a guard for Richmond. He eventually broke the scoring and assists records previously owned by his father—Ken Carter. Upon graduating from Richmond in 2001, Damien Carter received a full scholarship to West Point.

Ken Carter still lives in Richmond and remains close with his sisters...all seven of them. Carter continues to run the Coach Carter Foundation, the focus of which is education.